The Infinite Jeff
A Parable of Change

— Part 3 —
The Change

BY
Will Holcomb

will@willholcombauthor.com

ISBN 978-0-9916311-2-4
Updated: 8/16/2022
Amazon Version

Cover design by Jose Gomez

Amazon Paperback Edition

Dedication

I started *The Infinite Jeff* in 2010 with no idea what I was getting into. I had never written a book before. The first draft of the complete story took about six months of very late nights while having a family and a full-time job. The rough draft was the easy part. That was the fun part. Since then, that draft has gone through a massive number of edits. I wasn't a writer. My sister, Jackie, helped turn me into a writer. I dedicated Part One to her and my wife. When thinking about who to dedicate this part to, I want to thank and apologize to my children. For a long time, this book has eaten up a big portion of my attention and time. I believe *The Infinite Jeff* is an important book but Keaton, Landon, Dominic, and Joseph, all of you are so very important to me also. Thank you for your understanding and patience over the years.

Prelude

If you have not read Part One and Two of *The Infinite Jeff,* please do so now. Part Three is not a standalone story.

In Part One, Stanley, an out-of-work technical writer, has struggled to find a new job and find meaning in life. Of the three areas he feels should give meaning to life—family, work, and religion—he's realized that to find a job, he's going to have to leave the only one that has meaning to him, his family.

He gets a short-term contract job on the other side of the country. Too broke to fly, he has to drive. At the beginning of his cross-country road trip, he reluctantly picks up a hitchhiker, Jeff, who surprisingly is going to the same town as Stanley. As they drive, Jeff leads Stanley on a strange, life-changing adventure. Along the way, Jeff introduces Stanley to new concepts of religion and raises many questions about life.

In Part Two, Stanley finds a workplace that's totally different than anything he could have imagined. Instead of being a replaceable cog in the life-suck machinery of corporate America, he is seen by management and his peers as a unique individual offering something to the group no one else could offer.

Chapter 45

It was a nice cool Monday morning as I loaded up the Jetta. Jeff and I decided Monday was a good day to start our trip. This would give us plenty of time to get to Barstow for Sally's wedding the following Saturday. Really, Jeff asked if Monday was okay, and I had nothing on my schedule other than leaving, so I had no reason to offer a different timeline. It shouldn't take five or six days to drive to Barstow but I didn't protest. I'd learned Jeff didn't do things without reasons.

I'd spent the weekend after my going-away party, packing and cleaning up, and carting things I'd bought and didn't need at home to the local charity thrift store. I went to Jeff's church one last time and felt a deep loss. The probability of ever finding a church like this one was near zero. I finally got around to putting the "Invite the Change" decal on my rear window. For being someone who normally didn't like decals and bumper stickers on my car, I stood back and admired my work. It was good. By the time Monday morning rolled around, I'd run out of stuff to do.

Or I thought I had. I'd "mostly" loaded my car Sunday night, but the "little bit" I'd left for the morning, of course, wasn't as "little bit" as I'd thought. Then I had to do the final check-out inspection with the hotel folks, then I'd had to stop for gas, then I had to..., and then I had to..., just like every trip I'd ever gone on. I'd been hoping to be on the road by nine, but it was after eleven by the time I made it to Jeff's house to pick him up.

I opened the gate with my remote and drove up the drive with the uneasy feelings that came along with knowing this would be the last time. I climbed the polished granite steps leading to the magnificently carved door and paused before I knocked. I took a long look at the door and then the stairs and then turned back and looked at the driveway and sumptuous yard. I pretended I was taking mental pictures, making a spot in my brain to permanently hold the images I was taking in.

Yeah, I could have gotten out my cell phone and taken pictures, but I wasn't attempting to record the visual image. I wanted the emotions I'd experienced here, and the emotions I was experiencing now, recorded. Maybe Jeff could create a camera that did that, wouldn't that be cool!

The amusement that came with the thought helped me blink away the tears that threatened, and I turned back to the door, mostly dry-eyed.

As I raised my hand to knock, the door opened.

Jonathan beckoned me in, and I got the feeling he'd been watching me through the door's big side windows, waiting for me to be ready to enter.

When I crossed the threshold, I had enough time to hand Jonathan the remote before I was swarmed by kids and had my toes run over numerous times by the ones in wheelchairs trying to get close enough to hug me. What a wonderful house; it was always so lively, affectionate, and happy. Even though I'd spent most of my time in this house helping Dylan, I'd grown close to this family and would miss them greatly.

Grace stood to the side, watching with a radiant smile. When the path cleared a little, she worked her way in to give me a long hug and spoke kindly into my ear. "Thank you, Stanley. You've given me so much while you were here. It's wonderful having you as part of the family."

As I hugged this astounding young woman, I wondered what I'd given her. I started to ask the question, but she held up her index finger. "Uh-uh. Don't question. Trust me, you have."

"It was wonderful to be part of the family." I leaned forward to give her another hug but she stopped me.

"Was? There is no was here. You are part of the family."

I held up my hands beside me. "What was I thinking? I should have known it was a trap I couldn't escape."

Grace gave one firm nod. "Now you're starting to understand." She then leaned in to give me the hug she had interrupted.

There wasn't any doubt who her dad was. As she stepped away, I spotted Dylan, stoically leaning against one of the stair railings, waiting for the crowd to say their good-byes.

Once they stepped aside, in a slow and deliberate manner, he walked up to me and extended his hand. As I reached out and took his hand, in a calm, controlled voice he said, "Until I see you again."

I shook his hand and said, "Goodbye, Dylan."

He sternly corrected me, "No! Until we meet again. This isn't the last we'll see each other."

The kid was amazing. As I'd worked with him, I'd come to believe his IQ test was correct because he struggled with every intellectual step forward. But Jeff was right when he said Dylan's self-discipline, his positive attitude, and his drive, overcame what he lacked in intellectual ability.

"I like that much better, Dylan. Until we meet again." Then I pulled him in and gave him a big hug.

I had said goodbye to Marcus after the concert. He was a very busy man now with his new fame. So, it was extremely special he took the time to play at my going away party.

Jeff came down the hallway with his backpack and his suit for the wedding. After he hugged and kissed each and every kid goodbye, he pulled Jonathan in for a hug. You'd think Jonathan would be used to Jeff since Jonathan helped raise Jeff, but Jonathan hugged Jeff as stiffly as a stranger. Just for fun, I thought of hugging Jonathan, but restrained myself and shook his hand and said goodbye as Jeff and I walked out the door.

Jeff tossed his backpack in the car and placed his suit bag carefully over the top of the boxes. We both slid into our seats and buckled in. With many emotions bouncing around inside me, I started the car.

For better or worse, we were on our way.

I headed down his long drive for the last time and felt the spectrum of emotions increase as I watched the beautiful house recede in the rearview mirror.

After I turned onto the street, I had to ask, "Will this trip be anything like the trip here?" I wanted some hint as to what to expect.

Jeff smiled as he pulled out my Google Maps printouts which I'd inserted between my seat and the center console. He looked over them while saying, "Come on, Stanley! Where's your sense of mystery? Of adventure? Do you want an itinerary for this trip?"

"That would be great!" I replied with sincerity. I wasn't up to dealing with Jeff and his shenanigans after these emotional few days. "At least then I'd be somewhat prepared, so I can keep a lookout for trash cans to throw up in."

He opened the center console compartment and took out a pen, then looked at me. "I'll make you one promise."

"That's more than I was expecting to get from you."

"We won't stop at any malls to go shopping."

That comment brought one of the many questions that continued to nag me to the forefront of my mind. One that had tumbled around in the back of my mind since Jeff brought it to my attention. Where was humanity going to go with its economic model? But I quickly pushed it into the background; it wasn't anything I could answer while driving.

"That's way more than I expected," I answered, trying to lighten the mood. "I think I can handle almost anything else. Maybe this trip won't be so bad after all."

As I was saying that, my phone rang.

I took it out of the cupholder between the seats and looked at it with a mixture of disbelief and resignation. It was a number I didn't recognize. I hadn't gotten a single call for him since I dropped him off in that parking lot when we first got to Bethlehem a couple of months ago, and now, we hadn't been on the road five minutes, and Jeff was getting calls on my phone. I handed him the phone and he took it with a faux look of guilt.

"Hello?" he answered, then I could hear the welcome in his voice when he spoke again. "Hey, Luke!"

As I recognized the name, flashes of Luke and me at the drug house consumed my vision. The memory of Jeff standing at the front door of a drug house saying, "Luke's dad sent me here. He says Luke can't play with you guys anymore;" the memory of the gun at Jeff's head; the memory of the police raid, brought all the horror of that moment crashing back with Technicolor intensity.

The fear of those moments returned and it was only the fact that we were in heavy traffic that kept me from closing my eyes and concentrating on my breathing. The illusion that I was mentally prepared for the trip with Jeff was destroyed. Why had I agreed when Jeff suggested he ride with me to the wedding? I wasn't going to survive the trip home; he'd get me killed this time, I knew it, without a shadow of a doubt.

At least Sam had upped the value of my life insurance, so Beth and the kids would be taken care of.

"You have great timing, friend," Jeff said, interrupting my morbid thoughts. "Stanley and I will be in your area in a couple of days. I'm sure he wouldn't mind us stopping by." He turned to me. "Would you, Stanley?"

I looked at him, letting my feelings of horror and dread show on my face.

"No problem, Stanley's all for it," Jeff cheerfully replied, his expression full of laughter at my expense. "When we get closer, I'll let you know exactly when we'll be there." He hung up and placed the phone back in the cupholder.

I waited for him to fill me in, but he looked out the window and watched the trees go by. As my remembered emotions from my first meeting with Luke drained away, leaving a sense of inevitability, I reminded myself, "It's all part of the experience." But I wouldn't give Jeff the satisfaction of letting him know that, while I might not look forward to seeing Luke after the last experience, on some level, I hadn't felt the least bit of surprise when his name came up again. "So? We're stopping to see Luke?"

"Yep."

When he didn't say more, I gave an exasperated huff. "Well, how's he doing?"

Tilting his head to look at a billboard we were passing and then back to the map printouts. "He sounded like he was doing pretty well."

"Doing well, huh?"

"Yeah," he said placidly as he started writing on the maps.

Irritated with Jeff's games, I gave up. I wasn't going to play along.

As I made my way to the highway, Jeff was quiet, and my mind drifted in and out of scenes from our trip here.

After a few minutes, I looked over at Jeff. "Hey, do you think we can stop at George's bookstore on the way back? I really liked that place."

"Sure. I stop there anytime I'm close."

"That's cool." I reached over, turned on the radio, and searched for something to listen to. *"Car Talk"* with Click and Clack, the Tappet Brothers, was playing on the fourth station I tried.

Jeff's face lit up. "Oh! I love these guys. What a great way to start a trip."

I'd always liked them, too, and agreed that it was a great way to start a trip. We drove along listening, laughing, and trying to see if we could diagnose the car problems before Tom and Ray. I lost hands-down.

Chapter 46

As we drove through the day and into the evening, we made great time. That was the nice thing about traveling with another adult male, guys packed road trip food and drinks, and stopped only for pit stops when we needed gas. And with the six-hundred-mile range of my Jetta, we weren't stopping very often.

So far, Click and Clack had been the high point of the trip, and I was starting to think the invention of the iPod had killed all the radio stations along our route. While part of me was thankful for the smoothness of the trip so far, because I didn't want a repeat of carrying a flat tire in the rain, I was amused to discover that the other part of me was vaguely disappointed. I'd expected this trip to start with a bang, instead of this long stretch of boring miles.

No sooner had I thought that Jeff pointed at an exit. "Let's get off there."

Looking at him. "Really? Didn't we just stop?"

He gave a humored huff. "That was over two hours ago when we stopped for dinner. It's almost eight o'clock now, we've been at this for almost nine hours, and I want to stop for a bit and get my blood flowing through my legs again."

I needed to stretch, too, but I wasn't going to let him know that. I put the blinker on and took the exit.

As I pulled into the gas station Jeff directed me to, right off the exit, I looked around. It was your typical gas station, but there was something about this one that made me look around it again. It was nicely maintained, with a fast-food restaurant attached to the convenience store part, but we'd stopped at plenty of gas stations that looked pretty much like this one. What was it about this place?

Jeff interrupted my thoughts. "You want to fill up now or in the morning?"

"Guess we're here, might as well do it now."

I parked at a pump, got out, and we started to go inside to prepay. As we walked, I kept looking around trying to figure out why this place triggered my brain as it did. Above the door was an "*Invite The Change*" sign. That was cool, I thought. I glanced over towards the tire inflator as we got to the door and started walking through. A hint of memory popped into my head. "Hey, isn't this where we—"

"Jeff! Stanley!" a vaguely familiar male voice called out.

Quickly, I turned to see who could possibly be calling us. The cashier was waving at us, and my mind didn't even have to work to place him. The cashier waving was Derrick, the kid who'd given us a ride back to our car when we'd had the flat tire in the rain.

I can't say I'd consciously thought much about Derrick after he dropped us at our car, but as I looked at him behind the counter, tending to the short line of people waiting to be checked out, I realized our experience with him had subconsciously puzzled me. Of all the strange things that had happened with Jeff and me on our way out here, our time with Derrick was an anomaly. Jeff had helped everybody we met on the trip in some way, except Derrick. Jeff had done nothing to help Derrick.

We walked to the counter, and Derrick leaned over the boxes of gum to shake our hands. He looked at the next guy in line. "Hey, Vince. This is Stanley and Jeff. They had a flat tire here a couple of months back, and I gave them a ride." Vince shook our hands, and Derrick continued. "Vince, here, is one of our teaching greats. Each year, he takes a class of mindless sixth graders and transforms them into thinking human beings." Derrick then introduced us to the two other people in line in much the same way.

As Derrick continued to ring up the people in line, we all chatted, with Derrick leading the conversation with interesting bits of insight that left everyone amused and feeling good. And as new people walked in, Derrick greeted everybody by name and orchestrated a conversation that didn't leave anybody feeling like good manners obliged them to stay or that a newcomer was intruding, welcoming each coming and going as the conversation's natural flow.

After I'd been watching in amazement for a few minutes, another clerk came to the register, and Derrick looked at the clock over the entrance and remarked, "Oh, I didn't know it was that time already." He looked at Jeff and me and asked, "You guys in a hurry? I'd like to hear how the rest of your trip went."

Jeff looked at me to get my approval.

"Sounds fun." I wanted more time with this guy.

Derrick looked pleased. "Alright! Just give me a couple of minutes to do the shift hand-over."

The people in line said good-bye, and Jeff and I headed to the bathrooms which were shared by the store and the restaurant. As we walked I scowled at him. "Is there any reason you couldn't have said, 'Hey, Stanley, want to stop and see Derrick? He works at the gas station where we filled the tire up.' I would've said, 'Sure, Jeff, I'd love to see him. He seemed like a great guy.'" I held up my hands imploringly. "Is there any reason we can't have a conversation like that?"

Jeff turned to me and grabbed my shoulder. "Hey, Stanley, want to stop and see Derrick? He works at the gas station where we filled the tire up."

Sarcastically, I added, "Sure, Jeff, I'd love to see him. He seemed like a great guy."

He let go of my shoulder and patted it. "Cool. Have that out of your system now?"

"Yeah, I feel so much better." Then I grinned at him. "We've driven today for almost ten hours and nothing weird has happened. I was starting to worry the trip would be normal."

He jokingly elbowed me. "I know. I could feel your disappointment growing. I was thinking I'd have to come up with something before we got here, but you held off."

After we paid our dues to the Mt. Dew gods, and while waiting for Derrick, we picked up a few things and took them up to the new cashier. As usual, Jeff handed the new clerk a hundred-dollar bill to pay for the gas and our stuff and told him to use the change on the next people.

The clerk hesitantly took the bill as he looked at Jeff with a questioning expression. "What do you want me to do?"

Jeff explained again, and obviously doubting Jeff's sanity, the clerk reluctantly agreed.

As we walked away from the counter, Derrick exited one of the back rooms. The three of us headed to the door and walked to the Jetta.

We chatted as I filled up the car. Derrick asked about the trip two months ago and where we were heading now, and we filled him in. Then he laughingly asked if I'd remembered to check the spare tire this time, and I assured him that I had.

Leaning on the trunk of my car as we talked, I noticed a difference between how Jeff interacted with Derrick and how he talked with most other people. I found myself fascinated by the subtle difference in how Jeff responded to Derrick.

Jeff never talked down to people, but it was always clear to me that Jeff was—I tried to put it into words: far above? more advanced? beyond? I'm not sure what word best describes it, but Jeff's expression always held a knowing, as if he knew something others didn't know. He's like a poker player holding a royal flush. Or the face of the hero in a movie where the villain has the hero seemingly trapped, but the hero knows he has a secret escape route.

Yet, with Derrick, Jeff talked as if Derrick knew the secret, too, as if they were equals. If I would have tried to picture who Jeff might treat as an equal, a convenience store worker in his late teens would've been pretty far down the list. And it made me wonder what the secret was they knew, but seemed to elude everyone else?

The pump clicked off and I hung it up. I still wanted to figure out more about Derrick, so I pointed towards the restaurant part of the store. "I'm not too excited about getting back on the road yet. You guys want to get something in there?"

They both nodded in agreement. I pulled the car up to a parking spot near the door and they walked through the parking lot. As I watched them walk towards me, I focused on Derrick. Sure, he was an extraordinarily pleasant kid, but Jeff and I had run across people like that before. What was special about him?

At the counter, I ordered a milkshake and fries and paid for it. Derrick was next in line and greeted the cashier and asked about her school. Then he called back to a couple of the people working the grill. My food came before Derrick even ordered so I took my tray, found a booth, and slid into it.

From my vantage point, I could look through the large archway between the restaurant and the store, right at the store's counter. Curious, I watched the new clerk and the people now in line. When

Jeff and I had first walked in, the people in line were interacting with each other and Derrick like they were all old friends. Now, the clerk barely looked up, the people waiting in line were impatient, and no one talked more than necessary to conduct the transaction.

Shortly, Jeff and Derrick arrived with their food and slid into the booth seat across from me.

When they didn't start talking, I decided to try to learn more about Derrick. "How long you been working here, Derrick?"

"Almost three years now. My mom got sick back then, so I had to quit school and start working. I'm lucky this job came up when it did, or we'd have been homeless. They've been pretty good to me here."

His answer shoved my thoughts into two contradictory directions. In one direction, it was obvious that Derrick was a highly admirable person to have given up so much to care for his mom. In the other direction, I couldn't help but see Derrick as a high school dropout with low employment standards.

Sadly, my mouth took the negative path. "Good job?" I instantly regretted saying that.

He looked down meekly and smiled. "I know it's nothing compared to what you guys probably do, but yeah, it's a good job. I like what I do."

I wasn't going to risk another question, so I worked on sucking the milkshake through the straw.

Jeff, on the other hand, happily traveled right down that path. I'm sure he did it for me. "Seems like you have more to offer than this."

Derrick looked down again and didn't smile this time. He took a French fry and started lifting it towards his mouth but then stopped. With the French fry in his hand, he moved it slowly back and forth towards Jeff as he spoke. "I've thought a lot about that. But the thing is, I make a difference here. People come in here just to see me and talk to me. Sometimes I feel like I'm a minimum wage therapist. The couple who own the place are great, and I help them get business. They aren't getting rich off of this place, and they're raising four of their grandkids." He quit wagging the French fry and put it in his mouth. After he swallowed, he continued his thought. "The people who stand in that line every day are my friends. Any one of them would drop anything they were doing to help me."

A skeptical thought crossed my mind, and even though I tried to hide it, it must have shown on my face.

"I'm not just saying that, I know it for a fact. You know, just like that Christmas movie where the angel shows a guy what the world would be like if he wasn't there."

"*It's a Wonderful Life?*" I suggested.

"Yeah, that's it. Mom was getting sicker and it wasn't lookin' good. I didn't say anything, but somehow, word got out. Just like the end of that movie, money started pouring in from all over the place. We had buckets of money to pay for her medical treatment." He laughed as he thought about it. "It was hard to count because it was mostly crumpled one-dollar bills and jars of pennies people had been saving, but when you have that many people giving a little bit, it adds up fast."

As Derrick spoke, I started seeing a glimmer of what Jeff saw in him. This wasn't an ordinary kid motivated by ordinary desires. He saw things differently. I've always heard people talk about 'old souls' but never really knew what they meant. Yet, those were the words coming to mind with Derrick. He didn't sound like a boy in his late teens. He sounded like a monk who sat under a tree meditating on the meaning of life.

I said, "Wow! That's a wonderful story, Derrick."

He smiled shyly at me. "So, yeah, I guess I could do something else but I feel real good right here, and my mom's and my needs are met, in one way or another." He turned in his seat and pointed through the archway to the convenience store counter. "Look there. The lady checking out is on her cell phone and the others in the line are on their phones. It's like the guy behind the register's invisible." He turned back to face me. "It's like that almost anytime you look. But no one does that when I'm there. They all stop whatever they were doing before, and we connect for that short time. Even if they don't know me, I pause, I look them in the eye, I smile, and the funny thing is, they *always* put their phone away." He dipped another French fry and ate it. "I figure I make a connection with at least a hundred people a day. I look at them, they look at me, and we both feel better for having done it. Where else could I do that?"

It was starting to become clear Derrick understood something most people didn't; something that just recently, if I squinted very hard, was starting to take a fuzzy form in front of me. To him, the money he made at a job wasn't as important as the connections he made there. And because of those deep connections with the people here at the gas station, his and his mom's needs were met. This was someone I could learn from. I was probably twice his age and didn't know how to implement what he took for granted.

Thankfully, the conversation got lighter after that, because I wanted to think about the thoughts forming in the cobwebbed sections of my brain.

I focused on the two men sitting across from me. What did they have in common? What did they both get that I didn't get?

Glancing over their shoulders, I again looked at the customers at the convenience store register. Then I turned and looked at the line for the restaurant here. Almost everyone was on their phone or staring blankly into space. This brought back the memory of Jeff getting calls on my phone because he didn't have one of his own. When I'd asked him why on the trip out here, he told me he didn't like cell phones because they brought the rest of the world into that moment. On our trip, Jeff and I didn't talk the whole time, but anytime we talked, he was one hundred percent there.

Then I suddenly realized that I didn't have to search more for the answer because Derrick had already told me: connections. That's what he and Jeff had in common.

As I thought about it, that's what made HRI different. At HRI people didn't casually work with each other, they connected with each other, and I'd felt connected to everyone I'd worked with. I expanded my thought out to the other things I'd experienced. Rita and her class? I'd connected with them and was going to miss them. Jeff's church? I'd connected there on more levels than just the people. Jeff's family? Well, that connection was obvious and deep enough that I knew I'd never recover. Marcus and his 'The Change' project? It was all about connection. Everything I could come up with that Jeff touched was about connection.

I turned my thoughts in the opposite direction, to the other places I'd worked, to Beth's church, and the kids' school. And I couldn't come up with one meaningful connection I had in any of those places. Why was that? What were they doing wrong compared to the places Jeff touched?

Then, just like the countless times since this crazy journey began, it hit me. And I felt like such an idiot, I let my head fall forward and hit the table with a loud thud.

Jeff and Derrick fell silent.

Without looking up I said. "It's not their job to connect with me. It's my job to connect with them. They're not doing it wrong. I am." As I said this I wondered if this was the secret Jeff and Derrick shared.

I looked up and saw Derrick give Jeff a mildly worried look.

Jeff calmly said, "Don't worry. He does this every once in a while. It seems to be happening less though."

I looked closely at the two men sharing the table with me. I was truly in the company of greatness.

Chapter 47

We talked with Derrick some more but thankfully not too much because my mind was full. Jeff and I drove for about thirty minutes and stopped at a cheap roadside hotel before we got into Indianapolis. When we checked in, I placed my debit card on the counter. I wasn't stressed about money like I was on the trip here, so I didn't feel right mooching off Jeff.

Jeff turned and gave me a very rare serious look. "Stanley, knock it off. Take your family somewhere nice when you get back."

For a second, I thought about protesting, but his look caught me off guard so I gave in. I put my debit card back in my wallet.

Once in my room, I threw my travel bag into the chair and lay down on the bed. As the mattress springs poked me through the well-worn comforter, I realized it was going to be a long night, which would make tomorrow a long day.

I pulled my cell phone out of my pocket and hit Beth's number. Then I put it on speakerphone, laid it on the pillow beside my head, and closed my eyes.

"Hey, Stanley," my wife answered.

"Ten hours. I'm beat."

She gave a short laugh. "I'll bet. Any weirdness on the trip?"

I rolled over and faced the phone. "Most of the trip was mundane. The only thing that really happened was we pulled into the gas station where Jeff and I had filled up the tire when we had the flat. Ends up, Derrick, the guy who gave us a ride, worked there."

With a hint of sarcasm, Beth replied, "My! What're the chances?"

I grinned at that. "Exactly. Jeff wanted me to see him. There's something there. Something Derrick has that I'm supposed to learn. It has to do with connections."

"Connections?"

"Yeah. Derrick connects with people like no one I've ever seen. Well, except for Jeff. He's a convenience store clerk, yet when I saw the customers interact with him, it felt like more than the usual pleasantries. They paused and took notice of him, they connected with him. I think that's why Jeff looks at him differently, also."

We were both quiet for a bit, and then Beth repeated the word, "Connections. Hmm. You know, it's funny because you hear that word all the time, but when I stop to think about it, I realize I mostly use it in a trite way. I'm trying to think of anyone I really connect with at a deep level. I interact with a lot of people, but can't say I connect with them."

I thought about harassing her for not having me on the list of people she connects with. But in truth, I can't say we connect very often. We don't stop our busy lives and truly take notice of each other. So I let the comment pass and moved on. "Anyway, I have some thinking to do about it, but I can't wait to get home and see you guys. Can I talk to the kids?"

We talked for a bit, but I was falling asleep on them, so I had to end the call and get to bed.

* * *

In the morning, Jeff and I followed the same pattern we'd fallen into on our trip here. We walked to a restaurant close to the hotel and had breakfast before getting on the road.

Once we got in the car after breakfast, I pulled the Google map print-outs from beside my seat to see if we needed to do any special navigation through Indianapolis. As I looked at the maps, I had to grin. I'd totally forgotten Jeff had written something on the maps right after we'd started the trip. Come to find out, he'd written, "Stop to see Derrick," with an arrow pointing to the exit we'd taken to the convenience store.

By now this was exactly the type of thing I'd grown to expect from him. I gave a quick laugh under my breath. "Do you plan out all your spontaneity like this?"

He was leaning his seat back and without looking at me answered, "Pretty much."

Looking back at the map, I saw he'd crossed off the road I'd planned on taking today. Instead, he had us going north on Hwy 65 to Chicago with "lunch" written in. Then he had us heading back south on Hwy 55 to St. Louis.

"That's a heck of a detour for lunch," I said.

He gave me a sly look. "You in a hurry?"

I shook my head. We'd given ourselves plenty of time to get to Sally's wedding, so wasting half a day getting some lunch wouldn't get me home to my family any quicker. After the wedding would be a different story. Stoplights would be optional on the trip from Barstow to Bakersfield. But until then, I'd just let the trip be what the trip was going to be. Besides, I'm sure he had a reason, and hopefully, the reason wouldn't include a bar fight or a raid on a drug house.

* * *

When we approached Chicago, Jeff put away his book and watched the road and traffic. "Pull in here," he requested and pointed to a highway rest stop. "We can change here."

I made my way to the right lane to take the exit. "Change?"

He nodded but just watched the traffic. "Yeah, you know what Jed Clampett used to say?"

You got to love someone who uses "The Beverly Hillbillies" references. "You tellin' me this is a fancy sit down eatin' place?"

He took his gaze off the traffic and looked at me. "Yep, and we need our Sundee go ta meetin' clothes."

I laughed to myself as I pulled into a parking spot close to the entrance. Our suits were laid on top of all my stuff so they wouldn't be wrinkled for Sally's wedding. I slid them off my two months' worth of living necessities, handed Jeff his and we headed to the restrooms.

We took turns changing in the handicap stall. Since I hated traveling in suits, I'd done this exact same thing countless times for interviews or various other reasons. But as many times as I've done this throughout my life, I can never get used to it. The cool thing is, my millionaire friend didn't seem to mind in the least.

I was standing in front of the mirror doing my tie while Jeff changed. He came to the mirror beside me, and I looked over at him. "Wowsers! That's a great-looking suit. What brand is it?"

He adjusted his tie in the mirror. "No brand. It's custom-tailored. There's this guy I like who's an outstanding tailor. I like to support him, so he does all my suits."

I had to laugh at "all my suits" as I stepped back to look at myself, standing in my one-and-only suit, which I paid fifteen dollars for at a thrift store. I'd thought it was a great suit, but standing beside Jeff, I looked pretty low class. But considering I wear a suit once or twice a year, this was all I need. But man! He looked sharp.

Chapter 48

Jeff directed me through the Chicago streets, and I'd have to call it another miracle we didn't run into any traffic jams and got there with remarkable ease. We pulled up to the restaurant's valet parking, and I felt something against my hand as I started to get out. Looking down, I noticed Jeff pushing a hundred-dollar bill into it. Taking hold of the bill, I wondered what he was doing.

One of the valet attendants started our way, and I looked at the other cars either being taken by the attendants or pulling up behind us. There was a Bentley, top-of-the-line BMW, Mercedes, and a few other super high dollar cars. I looked sheepishly at my Jetta and wished we had at least washed it. As I looked around again, I knew washing my humble Jetta would have done nothing to match the grandeur of these other cars.

The attendant waited somewhat patiently while I looked around at the other cars. I looked at him and said, "Man, talk about feeling out of place."

He smiled, leaned in towards me, and in a quiet voice said, "My guess is you don't have as much ego to fill as some of these people. Besides, I like your decal. I don't see many of those here."

I looked at my *"Invite The Change"* decal, returned his smile, and dropped my keys in his hand. He gave me my ticket and got in the car. I started to walk away when I felt the money Jeff had given me in my hand. Quickly, I turned and knocked on the window. He rolled down the window and looked at me questioningly.

"Sorry, I almost forgot." I handed him the hundred-dollar bill.

I could almost see his thoughts as he looked at the money. The tip didn't match the car.

He started to say something but I interrupted. "Take good care of it." I ran my hand over the roof. "It's a classic. They don't build them like this anymore."

His teeth showed through his smile. "Right on." He held his fist through the window and I connected mine to it. "She'll be shining when you get her back." And he was gone.

I looked at Jeff. "Nice kid."

"The world's full of 'em."

We walked into the restaurant, and I eagerly looked around. I was excited because I'd never dreamed I'd be able to eat at a place of this caliber. Jeff walked up to the maître d' and explained we had a reservation for two.

No spontaneity here, I thought. He knows what he wants even if it seems random to me. I wondered when he made the reservation.

I gawked at the restaurant's design and decorations as we were ushered to our seats. It was a nice blend of modern and classic design. I wanted to stop and look at the paintings, but Jeff and the maître d' headed right to the table. We sat down, took the menus handed to us, and I eagerly looked it over. It wasn't long before my eyes were bulging.

I quietly voiced, "Jeff, this isn't right. There's no way we can pay this much for lunch, or dinner for that matter. We aren't going to get out of here for less than three- or four hundred dollars, and that's if I order water." I continued to nervously look at the menu. People who grew up like me can't even fathom spending money like this. We use this type of money to make car payments, not buy lunch.

"You don't have to order water. Now relax, Stanley. Enjoy the atmosphere. You'll like the food." He smiled as he tried to reassure me.

"Liking the food doesn't make any difference, Jeff. This just feels wrong to me. There has to be something wrong with spending this much on a lunch."

"Look around the restaurant, friend. Do these people look like they feel it's wrong?" He waited for me to scan. "You just didn't grow up in a world where people have money to spend. I can afford it, so don't worry."

Jeff was relaxed, so I tried to relax but felt very uneasy. I studied the menu to find something reasonably priced, but couldn't.

Jeff finally asked, "Do you want me to order for you? I guarantee you'll love what I order."

"Sure, I guess. But we can go if you want. This is way too much."

"Stanley, this is how the other half lives. Just enjoy it."

"The other half?"

"Okay, maybe the other one-percent but still…"

The couple at the table next to us ordered, and I scanned the menu to find what they ordered. Their appetizers were over one hundred dollars, entrées were a hundred-and-fifty dollars each, and the bottle of wine to go with the meal was one of the cheaper ones at one hundred ninety-five. Their bill added up to about the amount of the mortgage payment I was struggling with.

Quietly, I asked, "What do these people do for a living?"

He casually surveyed the room. "Some of them, nothing. There's lots of old money here. Others are CEOs of some major companies. You know, those top executives you seem to have such a problem with." He looked around more. "High-powered lawyers, some organized crime, stockbrokers, politicians, entrepreneurs of different sorts, and other stuff like that. Pretty much what you'd expect."

Uncomfortably, I tried to settle back in my chair. "They all seem so casual like this isn't a big deal. They're dropping money with just as much concern as I'd pay for lunch at a fast-food place, maybe even less."

The waiter came and Jeff chatted with the young man before ordering.

Not wanting to deal with the guilt, I didn't even look at the menu prices of what he ordered, so I just watched the people here in astonishment. How could they spend so much money for this, when so many people in the world struggle for the most basic daily necessities?

The waiter walked away once Jeff ordered, and after a minute, I noticed Jeff was watching me with his intense smile. I looked at him quickly, as he asked lightly, "Are you judging these people, Stanley?"

"No!" I defensively shot back.

He didn't respond, just looked at me, waiting.

I tried to find something else to focus on other than the people or Jeff's expression, but as I did, his question bit at me, begging to be re-answered. "Okay, yes, I am," I finally admitted. "But Jeff, look at this. It isn't right. I mean, how can this be right? There are so many people in this world in need. People who would benefit from the money here. But instead, it's being spent on over-priced lunches."

"So, because these people eat here, or have nice cars, or nice houses, they're not helping anyone?"

Realizing I was setting myself up, I decided to end the game. "Okay, I'm judging them and making assumptions, but don't play with me. What do you want me to learn?"

"You're short-tempered for having just started the trip, aren't you?" he jabbed in his typical playful way.

"Come on Jeff!" I whispered emphatically. "Just get on with it. Enlighten me so we can move on."

"There are so many ways to go with this one because it's such a tricky subject. Jesus said 'It is easier for a camel to go through the eye of a needle than for a rich man to enter the kingdom of God' for a good reason. Your presumption about many of the people here is spot-on. Some of them are self-centered, narcissistic jerks. But not all of them." He took a drink of water. "You remember our talk on the way here about people with money and about self-love."

"Sure."

"Almost everyone eating here has a lot of love for themselves, but there's a huge variation in how they define and implement that love. In Roberto Assagioli's book *The Act of Will*, he does a great job talking about a lot of stuff, and in one spot, in a few sentences he sums up two kinds of self-love. He says the two important things to consider about self-love are what we love in ourselves and how we love it. If we love our craving for pleasure, possessions, or domination, it's egotism. If we love our potential, our creativeness, our relationships with others, if we love what's good in us, then that is a worthy self-love."

Sitting back, looking at Jeff, I wondered what this lesson had to do with me. I reached for my water and took another look around the room and thought about the ways that these people might love themselves. Then I wondered how I loved myself.

Also, with a habit I'd formed lately, I mentally noted the book he mentioned so I could read it later.

How did I love myself? That wasn't a simple question.

Jeff continued, "So, you said the money here could be used to help others." He looked over towards the far side of the restaurant at a middle-aged couple. "That couple. They are both highly successful in their careers and the money is rolling in. They own a nice house, nice cars. He likes to sail and has a wonderful boat. She enjoys artwork and has a pretty expressive collection, and is personally aspiring in her own artwork. Interestingly enough, they carry no debt, so property taxes, insurance, utilities, you know, reoccurring stuff, are their only expense."

Discretely watching them interact with each other was heartwarming. He put some butter on a piece of bread, handed it to her, and then let his hand rest on the table as he leaned in to look at her. As she reached for the bread with one hand her shoulders rose slightly as she coyly cocked her head to the side and gave him an affectionate smile while laying her other hand on his.

Looking back at Jeff and with a bit of envious sarcasm, I said, "Man, his wife's going to be mad when she catches him with that woman." Maybe it's been too long since Beth and I had been out without the kids. We have a good relationship, but I couldn't remember the last time she looked at me like that.

Jeff laughed and looked back across the room towards them. "They've been married for twenty-four years."

Following Jeff's gaze back towards them, I said, "They look like a happy couple. You know them well? You run in the same circles with them?"

He shook his head. "Never met them."

I had no doubt what he said was the truth, yet I asked, "You just happen to know all those details? You just look at people and know all their past and their motivations in life?"

He gave me a nonchalant smile. "Maybe I'm just making it all up. Would that change things?"

For a moment I wondered if it would matter, then answered truthfully. "No, really it wouldn't. I guess that's no different than a parable. Go on, tell me about them."

Jeff continued his carefree smile. "The point I was making is they're both very good at making a lot of money and very good at managing their money. If they both lost their jobs tomorrow, they wouldn't be stressed at all."

I didn't say anything, but after recently going through losing my job and being stressed because I never managed my money well, I could appreciate what he was saying.

"The main thing that would bother them is cutting back on their giving, even though their lifestyle would be cut even more. They are extremely active philanthropists. If they were without an income and they couldn't give as much financially, they'd almost be happier. With their schedules now, they can't spend much time helping with the causes they believe in. But if they lost their jobs, they would happily go where they felt called to help."

I put my elbows on the table and leaned in towards Jeff. "That's cool. But right now, what they're paying for their lunch could do someone a lot of good."

He looked at me questioningly. "Would it? Would them taking all of their money and dumping it into a worthy cause be doing a lot of good?"

I knew where he was going. "No, I guess not."

"One of the worst ways to try to 'fix' things is to dump money into it. There are some extremely good people here with lots of money and are actively using their money to 'help' in ways they feel they can, but it's unrealistic to think they should blindly dump money into causes."

"Like you and the schools? Or, in fact, Marcus and *Invite The Change?*"

"Right, I put a lot of money into the schools, but I'm deeply involved, or have people I trust who are deeply involved. Being wealthy is a very hard thing to do well."

Trying to sum up what Jeff was saying I interjected, "So, in essence, you're saying, they put a lot of money into causes where they truly think they can help. So, them eating at a place like this isn't frivolous."

"And this is an outstanding restaurant. They appreciate it for its quality in the same way people appreciate art. There is a beauty in the world that can only flourish if it's supported. I have the privilege to help others in so many ways because of my money. One way is to help the needy, another is to support art and beauty."

The memory of Jeff putting on the suit in the restroom came to mind. The suit was an example of that. It supported a tailor he admired. I thought back to Jeff's house. That is exactly what his place was to me. It wasn't about showing how rich he was but instead expressing an artistic vision and supporting craftsmen who make a vision reality. As I thought about Jonathan telling me how Jeff's parents had the house built, I thought about his parents. "You grew up wealthy. Is this the world you grew up in?" I'd rarely thought about Jeff's upbringing. His parents were filthy rich, so he was the son of a filthy rich couple.

He shot me a look. "Come on, Stanley. What do you think? From everything you've learned about my parents in the Institute, from Jonathan or any place else, what do you think?"

He wasn't saying it angrily but yet sounded a little insulted.

"I'd never thought of it before now. You throw money around pretty freely but I'd never seen you spend much on yourself. In fact, I don't know if I've ever seen you spend money on yourself other than basics," I answered him.

"I'm just playing with you. My parents came to places like this sometimes. Like the couple there, they appreciate quality and were willing to pay for it. But in truth, my parents felt more comfortable in a soup kitchen serving the soup."

"Then why are we here? Why are you here?"

"We came here for the atmosphere. Today, I'm willing to pay for that."

I saw our waiter coming towards us with a couple of plates and wondered if they were ours. I was starting to get hungry so I was thankful when he stopped at our table and placed the plates in front of us.

After looking at my plate I looked across the table to Jeff's. "I don't think I can eat this. It's too pretty to ruin."

He grinned at me. "Yeah, presentation is important here. It's part of the art. But trust me, the food tastes even better than it looks."

I breathed in deeply through my nose to take in the amazing aroma rising from the plate. Then I picked up my fork and took one more look before I destroyed it. I hadn't listened when Jeff ordered but this was a fish dish of some type. It had fancy swirls of some sauce I didn't recognize. The vegetables were cut and formed into interesting shapes. My fork cut into the fish, distorting the swirls, and once the bite was in my mouth my olfactory sense and palate harmonized to extract the highest possible elation from a dining experience I have ever had.

Jeff watched my face contort into an exaggerated look of satisfaction. "Guess you like it, friend."

"Oh my gosh, Jeff. This is outstanding. Is this pleasure or fulfillment?"

He got his own look of satisfaction from the question. "It all depends on you. There can be pleasure without fulfillment but there can't be fulfillment without pleasure."

I nodded but said, "I'll think about that later but for now, just shut up. I want to enjoy this."

He responded by picking up his fork to destroy the visual art and turn it into a taste art.

As I ate, thoroughly enjoying the food, I watched the couple Jeff had pointed out. They projected a feeling of warmth I'd have ignored if Jeff hadn't put it into a different perspective. I looked around the restaurant and tried to look at each patron in a different perspective. Some were easier than others but it was hard to match the glow of the first couple. As I watched people, Jeff's statement, 'Being wealthy is a very hard thing to do well,' took on meaning. Granted, Jeff had given me perspective on the one couple, but he said he might have made it all up. So I watched others with the same story going through my mind or tried to make up my own story which would place them in a glowing light. It may have helped but not to a great extent.

"Can I interest you gentlemen in dessert?" I heard our waiter say.

"Sure," Jeff said without even giving me a chance to voice my opinion. The lunch was impressive so I was more than interested in trying their dessert. Jeff looked at me. "You like Tiramisù?"

I shrugged. "Had it once or twice. I remember liking it."

The waiter smiled at me. He knew I was out of place but gave me an accepting look. I was too mentally occupied with the restaurant and its patrons when we first got here to pay attention to him. 'Connections', I thought, 'Derrick took time to connect.' I looked at our waiter's name tag and then looked him in the eye. "What do you think, Mark? Tiramisù?"

Our waiter nodded as he looked me in the eye. "It's one of my favorites. I highly recommend it."

I looked over to Jeff. "We have an expert opinion. I'll go with that." I looked back to our waiter. "Thanks, Mark. By the way, that lunch was wonderful. Someone needs to be complimented."

Again, he nodded. "I'll make sure to pass that along." Then he left.

I was about to comment on Jeff's dessert choice but a boisterous group of five were seated at the table next to us, drawing my attention. Their volume made it impossible not to eavesdrop. I literally heard statements like, "Why shouldn't I make more than most people? I'm smarter than them." Words like "deserve" and "owed" were laced throughout the conversation by all five people at the table. It was like they were talking just loud enough for us to hear and be impressed with their cars, houses, private planes, vacations, etc.

Across the restaurant, I watched the couple Jeff and I had observed toward the start of our meal chat pleasantly with their waiter as the man signed the receipt. Then they gracefully got up from their table and made their way out. There was an overwhelming elegance to the couple. I couldn't hear anything they said to the waiter but the smiles and body language of all three told of a pleasant and friendly relationship.

It was hard to appreciate the tranquility of that moment with the table next to us. I saw Jeff watching me but he didn't say anything and didn't have time. Our dessert was brought to us surprisingly fast. We thanked the waiter and exchanged smiles but I watched his smile vanish when he approached our neighbor table. He treated them politely but they didn't return the gesture. They gave their drink orders and then promptly acted as if he was gone.

This changed the meal for me. The atmosphere quickly turned sour. We ate in silence as I tried to block out the noise.

Jeff started speaking and I noticed him look at that layered dessert resting on his fork. "It's interesting. If you put too much or too little egg yolk in or don't beat it to the right thickness the dessert is ruined." He took a bite and then cut another piece and looked at it. "The mascarpone is important too. If you don't understand how all the ingredients work together, you can totally mess this up."

I narrowed my eyes and looked at him in confusion. "This isn't a cooking lesson, is it? You're trying to make some point."

He looked over at the loud table next to us, and then back to me. "Might just be a cooking lesson. Have you ever tried to make Tiramisù?"

Looking at the last bite of cake on my fork I tried to think about what point he was trying to make, but the people next to us made thinking hard. The decadence, the arrogance, the sense of entitlement from them was contaminating the fine experience I was having.

Our waiter came to the table. "Will there be anything else?"

Jeff held out his hand for the folder with the bill but didn't open it. "No, I think we are done. We have a long drive ahead of us so we had better get going."

The waiter gave an understanding nod. "It was a pleasure having you here today. Have a safe trip."

Nonchalantly, Jeff put some hundred dollar bills in the folder and started to stand. "Thanks. Stanley's a good driver. I'm in good hands."

"Come back and see us," said the waiter.

With that, we removed ourselves as an audience from our neighboring table.

Chapter 49

We left and the valet, the same attendant who took it, brought my humble Jetta around, handing me the keys.

I looked at my car and then the attendant. "Man! That looks great. I don't think it looked that clean when I bought it."

He gave me a look of gratitude. "Told you I would."

"Yeah, but at most I expected the top layer of dirt to be taken off not to have it detailed." I know Jeff had given me money to tip him before and I wasn't sure what the custom was but didn't care. I was thankful for the great job he did and he struck me as a great kid. I took out my wallet and took out a couple of twenties.

With a smile, the kid backed away and pointed. "Go up a block. There's this old guy that is always at the corner, army surplus clothes and all. I've gotten to know him a bit since I've worked here. He could use that more than me right now. You already tipped me enough."

Derrick popped into my head. When Jeff and I had met him the first time, Jeff said offering him money would have cheapened what he did for us. This kid seemed to have some Derrick qualities. I held the twenties, put my wallet away, and extended my empty hand. "Thanks again and it was great meeting you. Hope the rest of your day goes well."

He shook my hand. "Have a safe trip."

Jeff and I got in the car and pulled out onto the street. "Yeah, really nice kid."

Jeff patted my shoulder and repeated what he said when we walked into the restaurant. "The world's full of 'em."

We stopped at the light a couple of blocks up and I saw a man with a torn, green army jacket and a dirty gray, knotted beard. I handed Jeff the two twenties. Jeff rolled down his window and motioned for the disheveled man to come over.

With a stooped back and slight limp, he shuffled over. His eyes lit up when he saw the two twenties. He bent lower to see both of us and through rotted teeth said, "Thanks."

As the man reached for the money from Jeff, Jeff placed his other hand on top of the beggar's filthy fingers and held them with both hands for a brief moment. "Have a wonderful day."

"This will sure help. And you two have a good day, too." He stood tall and quickly walked away.

As I watched him leave something struck me as odd but I couldn't place it.

The old man suddenly stopped before getting to the sidewalk and in one motion turned back to us. "What ..."

Jeff pointed ahead of us. "Light's green."

The car behind us honked so I let out on the clutch and didn't get to hear the rest of the man's sentence. Did Jeff just... I looked over at him to say something but I knew him well enough now to know by the way he was already acting distracted, looking out the window, that was his way of telling me I wasn't going to get an answer. I let it drop.

I was about to head to the highway out of Chicago but Jeff started giving me some directions. Soon we were at the opposite extreme of the luxury car laden restaurant. Rundown buildings with broken windows, hookers watching us drive by to see if we were slowing down, drugs being sold barely removed from plain sight. I checked to make sure my doors were locked. That was a pointless effort because right after I locked them he had me pull over and park along the street.

The stench of urine offended my nose when I exited the car. As I made my way around the front of the car I looked up towards the building wall and the man with his back to us. I stepped past the stream of liquid flowing from his vicinity and onto the sidewalk.

Still, in our suits, we started walking and passed a bum asking for money. I walked a few steps before I realized Jeff stopped and was chatting with him and handing him a bill. I assumed it was a hundred-dollar bill since I'd never seen Jeff have anything but hundreds.

I waited for him and when Jeff caught up I asked, "Is giving him money a good idea? Won't it just be spent on alcohol or worse?"

Jeff shrugged. "Maybe. I don't know. Maybe it will help him out for a bit."

I just thought about it without responding. About a block later, in front of a boarded up building covered in graffiti, a couple of ladies offered us their companionship. Jeff stopped and held out a couple of hundred dollar bills. "No, we're not interested in that but would you do me a favor?"

The two women looked at the money and then looked at each other. Finally, the one to our right put her hand with long bright pink fingernails on her hip to rest at the top of her short denim skirt. "What you thinkin' about, baby?"

Jeff took a pen and paper out of his pocket and wrote something down. "All you have to do is promise to call this number and tell them Jeff told you to call." He held up the money.

The lady with the pink fingernails spoke again. "Just call a number? You gonna give us that money for calling a number?"

Jeff calmly answered, "That's it. Just call the number." He didn't wait for the answer and handed them the money and the paper. "You ladies have a nice day." He turned and started walking before they could ask more questions.

But I had the chance to ask. "Who's the number for?"

"I know a lady out here who runs a woman's shelter. She was on the street herself at one point in her life. Now I help support her organization to help women in these situations find a way out. The organization gets them training and medical help. It reaches out to their families to get them help if they will accept it also."

We walked in silence for half a block as I thought about that. I turned and looked at the women. The same one who talked to us was looking at the paper and dialing the number. I turned back. "Hope they can get the help. Hope they ..." I stopped talking when I saw a group of men congregated around the cement stairs leading into the building ahead of us. Their eyes followed us suspiciously as we grew closer.

I tried to act as calm as Jeff but the way they watched us scared the crap out of me. One stood and took a step towards us and I resisted the urge to hold Jeff's arm, figuring that wouldn't help my situation at all. Jeff kept walking calmly and the man just took a drag from his cigarette and watched us.

There was a group of men leaning against a car, drinking beer and smoking cigarettes. Jeff walked right up to them and leaned up against the car with them. I stayed back a few feet, not sure what to do. I wanted to run, but being with Jeff was by far the safer choice. I don't know if it would be called a prayer but my mind was asking that this not be a repeat of the drug house with Luke.

Jeff asked, just like he was saying 'hi' to someone in a grocery store. "Hey guys, how're you doing?"

Still, in our suits, they must have thought we were police or something because they tried to act calm. "Nut'en, man. Wa'cha wan?"

Jeff crossed his arms. "Just wanted a quick chat. Nothing much. You aren't in trouble or anything so just relax."

Man, Jeff was cool, he didn't look nervous at all. He's always got the royal flush.

"We aren't police or anything like that. Just a couple of guys."

I don't know what the politically correct term for their dialect is, but it was such bad English I had problems understanding them.

The one who seemed to be the leader said, "So aks yo queshun."

Out of the blue, Jeff asked, "How's the job search going?"

The leader didn't seem bothered by the question but instead seemed to enjoy the opportunity to complain about his situation. "Man, dey keep saying dey gonna get us jobs but dey ain't do'en nofin. All we's got'st ta do now is hang out here and drink beer. If dey would get us jobs we'd have sumfin ta do."

"How are you making it without a job?"

"Man, you know dat. Dey give us money but it ain't 'nuf. How can I support my kids wif as lil' as dey give me?"

"I see," replied Jeff. He paused for a bit and looked around the area. "You know, this isn't a bad place. I think if you guys put some time into cleaning up around here and fixing some of the buildings it could be nice."

"Man, we complained ta da city but they isn't doin' nufin. How we 'pos ta live like dis?"

Jeff again changed the direction. "I'm hearing a lot about *The Change*. What do you think of him?"

"Man, he great. Finly sum'un look'in out fo us."

"Well, it was great talking to you guys. Good luck finding a job so you don't have to hang out here."

"Lata," the guy who did most of the talking replied.

Jeff started walking away and I followed his lead. "What was that about?" I asked. "You just took me to two extremes."

"Did you notice something in common?" he inquired. "Think about the people at the table beside us."

Something in common? I thought. What would those two groups have in common? The arrogance of the table next to us was overwhelming but that wasn't the case with the people we just left.

We made our way past the group of people at the stairs as they eyed us suspiciously. But I was focusing on the van up the road from us. A couple of women got out along with a man. The man leaned against the front of the van but the two women walked up to the woman Jeff had given the money and the number to call. There was a short discussion that ended before we got there. All five people got in the van and drove away.

"That was fast," I remarked.

"Yeah. They don't waste time when it comes to getting women in need to safety."

The brake lights of the van came on as it slowed to take a turn and then it went past some dilapidated buildings and was out of sight. "That's great you're able to do that for them." I looked around for the man Jeff had handed a hundred-dollar bill to but didn't see him. "What about the guy? Where is he?"

Jeff turned and looked around. "Not sure."

I looked at Jeff as he looked around, pretending to be a normal person and not knowing where the guy was. "Was that a good idea giving him all that money? Most likely it's going to go to drugs or booze."

We got to the Jetta and I stepped over the discolored part of the sidewalk from the dried urine. Jeff placed his hand on the door handle and looked at me over the top of the car as he spoke. "It's a good question. Did I help him? But how many people aren't helped every day because people ask that question and then don't act because of that question?"

I was watching him over the top of the car but then pulled the handle, opened the door, and got in as I thought. He had a good question. How many people have I missed the opportunity to help for that exact reason? I put the key in the ignition and started the car. "I don't know."

* * *

Once back on the road we quickly found a place to change out of our suits and into clothes more suitable for a road trip. I was back in my shorts and a Spiderman T-shirt. With Chicago receding in my rearview mirror I thought about Jeff asking what the two groups had in common. I thought about the people at the table next to us and then the men standing by the car. What did they have in common? No answers were leaping to the surface of my cerebral cortex.

Before the number of telephone poles between us and Chicago grew into triple digits we had fallen back into our routine, I drove with an occupied mind and Jeff read.

He broke the silence as if a thought just popped into his head. "Remember hurricane Katrina and Rita in 2005?"

"How could I not? I watched the news about New Orleans for weeks after Katrina pummeled it. It was awful to watch."

"Yeah, it was pretty bad. Some of the people from the Institute volunteered at relief shelters in New Orleans and then they did that again when hurricane Rita came through the Texas coastal area."

"I can see HRI doing that."

He shook his head. "HRI didn't. People from HRI did. The company just willingly afforded them time but it was set up by individuals."

I nodded. "I can see that too. They are cool like that. I remember the relief effort didn't go all that smooth. The government handed out cards with a couple of thousand dollars but that didn't go as planned."

He went on. "Right. People from the Institute came back with stories telling that in the relief shelters for Katrina, many of the victims went on shopping sprees and bought flat-screen televisions, stereos, and all sorts of things like that. Then they came back to the shelter and waited for the volunteers to get them food and then waited for the volunteers to clean up the dishes, deal with the waste, and other tasks. At the Rita relief shelters, as soon as the victims got there they asked the volunteers where the kitchens were, asked for help getting supplies and started organizing work details, and worked alongside the volunteers to get people fed, clean the shelters and take care of the people who needed help. With the money, they got what they needed to get by until they could get on their feet."

He paused and waited for me to respond. My mind tried to predict where this was heading but no path was evident, so I just added my thoughts to the conversation. "Yeah, I'd heard stories about how bad the New Orleans relief effort went and heard stories about the two-thousand dollars being abused. But now that I'm thinking about it, I don't recall hearing as much about the Rita victims. Guess I attributed that to the destruction not being bad enough or hurricanes not being the money making news of the day."

"You're being a bit cynical about our news agencies, aren't you?" Jeff said it blandly enough I wasn't sure if he was serious or sarcastic.

"Of course I'm being cynical. Shouldn't I be? I mean, if the recovery effort at Rita went well, the best the news could do is run a few humanitarian stories. But if people weren't getting murdered or the relief centers weren't a health risk because trash and human waste wasn't being disposed of, or any of the other failings of the Katrina relief effort which were reported extensively, then it wasn't news."

Jeff rested both hands on his book and looked out the windshield. "Hmmm… I see."

He was quiet for a while and looked to be thinking as he watched traffic. Obviously, he brought all of this up for me to make some type of connection. So I mentally replayed the story he told of Katrina and Rita, and then tried to connect it to other events I experienced with him. A slide show of images started playing in my mind's eye. Some went by quickly as I dismissed them for lacking relevance but others slowed down as I tried to overlay that image with Katrina and Rita. One set of images kept repeating; the guys standing by their cars drinking beer.

Finally, the connection was made. "So, just like the guys standing by their car, it was somebody else's job to find work for them, clean up the neighborhood or fix the buildings."

"Exactly! Now, what's the difference between New Orleans and the Texas area?"

I thought for a moment. "I don't know. I don't know much about that area of Texas. My times in New Orleans I have always been struck with the run-down houses in some areas. Seems like the poverty is more out in the open. Is that part of Texas like that?"

He shrugged his shoulders, "Realize we're making some heavy generalizations but using the terms of an article I read, 'New Orleans is a victim of being in a welfare state.' They have a much higher welfare population. With the best intentions, the government helped create a culture of entitlement."

He paused for a minute and I had a thought just on the tip of my head wanting to spring out at any moment. It was almost there; I could feel it. It didn't come but the void was filled with another thought. "They have a victim mentality."

Jeff shrugged, "Maybe the government has created victims."

"Come on, Jeff. I'd expect you to promote a different idea. We set our own path or make our own future. Something like that. Not buy into victim mentality."

I was watching the road ahead but saw him look over at me. "You were recently unemployed and getting government help."

I got defensive at that statement. "That was unemployment insurance which I paid for my entire working career! As soon as I could get off of it I did."

Taking my eyes off the road I looked towards him as he nodded his head in affirmation. "Yes, you did. But during your unemployment couldn't you have taken some other jobs? You were a teacher before; you could've substitute taught during that time."

Again I defended myself. "I looked into that. But that would've counted as income and brought down my unemployment check the same amount I earned. I was better off using the time to look for a job."

"So you opted to take the government's money instead of earning your own?"

I knew I was being set up but continued down the path. "Yes, but what sense would that make? I was better off using my time to look for jobs. If I took any paying job during that time it would have counted against my unemployment income and just wasted my time. I was better off not working. I had money and time."

A grin filled his face. "You were better off not working?"

A feeling of dread gripped my stomach as soon as I realized what I said. Quickly I tried to backtrack. "I was... No, I mean... It wasn't like I was..." I quit and stared at the road ahead.

"You stuck with it until something better came along. Fortunately, you had skills provided from your education and so something better felt reachable. What would you have done if there was no hope of something better?"

He had trapped me and I wanted the focus off of me. "I know where you're going. But people get out of the welfare trap. There's training and grants for education. There are programs to open doors for people."

"And some people escape the drudgery of being a worker bee and become CEOs, ruling the hive. While others never aspire past their upbringing. You were fortunate enough to be born into a class with more open doors yet you haven't climbed past that class. Are you a victim?"

I huffed, "Okay, you've twisted my words and trapped me. So now what? Tell me what you want me to learn from this."

He gently punched my shoulder. "Those gentlemen we met today standing by the car have no easy way out. The odds are against them. Their environment's against them. They learned what they were taught. Only a gifted few rise above their environment."

A big truck belching black smoke made its way off the acceleration ramp into my lane. I looked in my driver-side mirror, then over my shoulder, and switched lanes. Jeff stayed quiet while I got around the truck and moved back into the cruising lane.

This gave me a minute to think. I switch off the blinker and said, "Gifted. Like Marcus."

Jeff almost laughed. "Yes, he's gifted but if he hadn't had intervention his gift would have caused a lot of people pain. His path was to go to jail, get out of jail, become an extremely successful gang leader, go back to jail, and be murdered."

I tried to mix that image with the Marcus I knew. The two didn't fit together at all. He was close to one of the most compassionate people I'd ever met. And now he was — my thoughts transitioned into words — "using the opportunity he was given to provide intervention for others."

"He's going to make the old way harder than the new way."

A jolt of energy shot through me. "Buckminster Fuller — You never change things by fighting the existing reality. To change something, build a new model that makes the existing model obsolete."

He patted my shoulder. "Love that quote. The model used to be that the community and churches helped people in need of help. With the community and churches doing it, to a greater degree, they're able to help people but didn't enable them. If the people weren't willing to help themselves out of their situation, then the community would start shutting them off. But now, the churches, like the government with all their best intentions, are the enablers."

For the first time, I disagreed with Jeff. I was pretty excited. "I don't know, Jeff. Beth's church was ready to help us while I was laid off. I don't think they would've ended up enabling us."

He nodded in agreement. "You said they were ready to help you out. Why didn't they?"

"We didn't need it yet but it was getting close."

"The model works well there. When churches help members of the church it's a blessing for everybody involved in most cases. But the model breaks down in many cases when the church feels obligated to help others in the community. This would be a good thing except that the others in the community many times are not part of the community, but instead, users of the community. They live off the community and don't give anything back. In these cases, the churches are just helping to enable these people."

"The churches are trying to help. You can't hold them at fault for that." I was surprised to hear myself defending churches to Jeff.

"You're absolutely right, friend. They're trying to help people and they should, but as we stated before, truly helping people is a very difficult thing to do."

"Dumping money into problems doesn't fix them." I quoted him from the restaurant.

"Exactly, they may need money but it needs to be used wisely."

"Again, like you at the school."

"Right, because I'm giving them money, I have a say in how the money is used. I'm very careful not to mandate any of my ideologies as a stipulation for the money. All I mandate is thought and work goes into how to use the money. I'm on a board there that looks at the research going on and I suggest ideas for the research. It is due to me that the school has no grades but I didn't mandate it. The board and researchers thought the idea merited exploration and they took it on as an area of research."

I heard a quick honk of a horn and checked my driver's side mirror to see what was happening, hoping my tire wasn't going flat or something else wrong. The car pulled up beside us and with smiles, the passenger and driver both gave me "okay" signs as they passed. Confused, I smiled and waved at them. As they pulled into the cruising lane in front of me I saw the "*Invite The Change*" bumper sticker. They obviously liked my decal.

I looked at Jeff. "That's cool."

With a satisfied look Jeff said, "Yeah, that is."

Looking back out the front window I returned us to the interrupted conversation. "But you were saying; stipulation, mandates, research, no grades, etc."

"Right. If I had dumped a bunch of money on the school and said, 'do what you want,' there'd be closets filled with learning aids for dust mites and the school system would be just as ineffective as before I gave the money. Throwing money at a problem is never an answer. Money is a tool and needs to be used in the correct way as part of a solution to a problem but money itself won't fix a problem and in most cases only makes it worse."

"That makes sense." From what I saw at the school, a lot was going on that was not Jeff's doing other than he made it possible with his money. But the programs had the thought behind them.

We drove along as I let this work itself through in my mind and tried to get that other thought to the front. Jeff had said something which had more meaning to it than he gave. He triggered something in my mind but I couldn't get it out and it was bugging me. We weren't talking so he reached over to turn on the radio but I stopped him. "I'm thinking."

"Okay," he said, reopened his book, and started reading.

He had taken me to those two different worlds, only miles from each other, and asked what they had in common. I'm pretty sure he gave me the answer but I, for the life of me, could not get that thought to the place in my brain which would let me say it. After about an hour I figured I needed to give my brain a break. "You can turn on the radio if you want."

He looked up from the book and said, "It'll come to you, friend." He reached over, turned on the radio and we simply listened to music as we uneventfully drove most of the rest of the day until I needed to take a break from driving.

Chapter 50

I pulled into one of those massive gas stations with row after row of pumps. My plan was to stretch and get something to munch on but then I saw an orange Lamborghini pull up to a pump. I jerked my wheel in that direction and said to Jeff, "Let's get some gas while we're here."

Jeff's eyes were locked on the same car as mine. "I'm with you on that, friend."

I pulled up to a pump next to the Lamborghini and tried not to stare as I got out. I've always had a fascination with those cars. The Lamborghini's door opened in its very cool vertical way and the driver stepped out, slid his card in the pump, and picked up the nozzle.

Jeff walked around to my side of the car and openly stared. We needed to go prepay for gas so I reluctantly started towards the store but Jeff walked over to the man. "Hello, friend."

The man looked over the top of his sunglasses with the unique Ray Ban logo on the lens and gave a small nod but said nothing.

Sometimes people just strike me wrong and this was one of those times. I felt guilty for judging him, especially after Jeff's comment in the restaurant. But this guy would have fit right in with the table next to us. It was like the car, the sunglasses, the clothes he wore, made him somebody.

Jeff was not going to be ignored. He walked up closer to the man. "Nice car, friend."

The man looked over casually and impersonally replied, "Thanks." But the man appeared uncomfortable as Jeff closed in on his personal space.

"It seems you and my friend own cars from the same company." Jeff continued even though it was obvious the guy didn't want to talk to us.

"What?" said the man in the Ray-Bans.

"Volkswagen bought Lamborghini in 1998. So technically you're both driving VW's. You guys are like kindred spirits."

He looked at my car with a sense of disdain. That made me angry. I like my car and it's served me very well even without the very cool doors. And it was still shining nicely from the detail job at the restaurant.

Jeff continued, "So, what engine do you have in it?"

"It's a V12," answered the man with an air of pride but a sense of annoyance.

"V12! Wow! That's big. How many liters is that?" quizzed Jeff.

"I don't know." Now the man was just irritated.

"Is this model fuel injection or carbureted?"

"I don't know." He was getting more irritated.

"I read these are mid-engine cars. What does that even mean?"

Now clearly irritated, he hung up the gas handle with a hard thud and crossly glared at Jeff. "Look buddy, I need to go. If you have all these questions, go look them up." The Ray-Ban man jumped in the car, closed the vertical door, and roared away.

Jeff turned to me smiling. "Well, what do you think of that?" He scanned the parking lot.

I had to smile at my wit as I replied, "His door is more vertical than he is."

Jeff stopped his scan of the parking lot to look at me with his approving smile. "Excellent, friend." Then he continued his scan until he saw what he was looking for. There was another one of my dream cars, a vintage Porsche 911 Turbo. "Come on," he motioned me to follow him.

Jeff started the conversation the same way as the horizontal man. "Nice car, friend."

The guy turned while removing his Ray-Bans to better see who was talking to him. "Hey, thanks," he replied with a smile.

Jeff pointed over to my Jetta. "It seems you and my friend own cars from the same company."

The Porsche driver looked over at my average car. "Is that a TDI?" he asked.

Jeff looked at me, so I answered, "Yes, it is."

"Cool, VW did a great job with those. I think old Ferdinand Porsche would've been proud. I don't understand why diesels don't sell better in the States. They get better gas mileage than most of the hybrids but none of the attention. What kind of mileage do you get with that?" he questioned with genuine interest.

"About forty-five," I answered.

"Whoa, that's impressive. I just don't get why those don't sell better." He was shaking his head and looking at my car.

Jeff brought it back to the man's car. "Yours is quite a beauty. The turbo ever give you problems?"

"Funny you should mention that. It went out about a month ago. A buddy of mine and I spent a couple of weekends rebuilding it. Neither one of us had ever been inside one of those, so there was a lot of trial and error but we got it working."

"I'll bet there was," Jeff replied. "Well, we won't keep you. Just wanted to come and appreciate your car, friend"

The man extended his hand to shake ours. "No problem, it's always nice to share a few words with some people who can appreciate these things. Don't forget to get your timing belt changed at 100k. It's a mess if you don't."

It dawned on me as he was saying it, I'd not thought about that lately. "Thanks for reminding me. I need to do that soon."

"You should have said something when we were at the Institute. We could've changed it," Jeff said.

"I've been pretty distracted lately, Jeff. You know that. It totally slipped my mind." I was wondering why the man who can predict the future didn't remind me I needed to do that.

The guy with the Porsche said, "That's an interference head. If that belt breaks you're going to have some serious work to do on the car."

I replied, "I know. Now the rest of our trip I'm going to just be waiting to hear the valves smashing into the pistons. That's going to take some fun out of the trip worrying about that."

"Well, good luck, hope you don't hear that," said the Porsche driver.

"We should be good but thanks for reminding me," I responded.

"Glad to do it. You guys take care. It was a pleasure talking to you." He got in his car and headed out.

As we were heading to the Jetta I said to Jeff, "What a nice guy. It's nice to talk to someone like that, someone who appreciated his car and could appreciate my car."

"What about our friend with the Lamborghini?" he inquired.

"Oh, him? Could care less if I ever talked to him again. I was glad when he drove off."

"What's the difference?" Jeff asked.

We were walking in to prepay as I pondered his question. "The guy with the Porsche had the car because he appreciated it. The guy with the Lamborghini had the car because he wanted to be appreciated," I finally answered.

"And how'd that work for them?"

"Pretty much the opposite."

"Funny world, isn't it?" Jeff said with his smile.

"Even the Ray-Bans had a different meaning to them. It's like the first guy was using them to impress people. The second guy took them off right away when he saw us so he could interact with us better. He had the Ray-Bans because of their quality, not the status."

We picked up a few snack items and Jeff left his $100 bill at the counter, we pumped our gas and left. One of these days I would like to hang out at the gas station and see how people react to that.

As we made our way to the highway I was thinking more about my very strange traveling companion. I knew enough to know it wasn't chance that two of my all-time favorite cars happened to be at the same gas station. What did Jeff want me to learn from them? I couldn't afford cars like that so my motivation to buy something so expensive is a moot point. Heck, I couldn't even afford the sunglasses they were wearing.

Chapter 51

We stopped for the night about an hour before St. Louis. Once in my room, I gave Beth and the kids a call and reported the day's happenings. She was mildly jealous of the lunch I had but that was about it. Mostly she and the kids were excited I was coming home.

After talking to them I got a book and started reading before I went to sleep, which wasn't long. My mind was tired from the driving and the thinking. Other than the venture into the Chicago slums, the day wasn't as stressful compared to the trip here. But it left me with plenty to think about with Jeff's question about what the two groups have in common. I drifted off to sleep trying to make a connection between the two groups.

I shot straight up in bed. I had it! I figured it out! I looked at the clock as I threw on my pants. It read 2:27. I went out my door and pounded on Jeff's door. I was slightly shocked when he opened the door soon after I knocked and looked too awake for this time of night. My wondering why he looked so lively at this hour almost pushed out my original reason for rushing over here. I yelled, "Entitlement!"

"You got it, friend. Come on in." He waved me in with a motion of his hand.

I entered and Jeff pointed to a chair by a table for me to sit in. He sat in the chair opposite me, moved a book from the chair's arm, and set it on the table. He had obviously been reading when I came which would explain why he got to the door so quickly and looked awake. Glancing at the bed I noticed it was still made so he hadn't gone to sleep yet.

Pushing all of that aside, I brought my mind back to the reason I rushed over here. "It's entitlement in different ways, but it's still entitlement." I was pretty excited. "The guys standing out by their car felt someone owed them something. They felt entitled to what they thought 'They', whoever 'They' is, owes them. The obnoxious people at the restaurant felt entitled to meals like that, cars like they drove or other things because of their titles, size of their bank accounts, intelligence, status in society or some other reason."

"So, what about you? What are you entitled to?" he asked.

My excitement vanished. I sat in his hotel room chair thinking about it for a minute and then got up and walked out to my room to think about it. I didn't even say goodbye; I was only wondering what I felt entitled to.

I grabbed the door handle to my room and realize I didn't take my key with me. Meekly I knocked on Jeff's door. "Left my key in my room."

He gave me an amused smile and walked out with me, grabbed my door handle, and opened the door.

"Thanks." It struck me odd that it didn't strike me odd Jeff could do this. I simply expected he could.

"No problem. Get some sleep. We have a long trip ahead of us."

It took me a while to get back to sleep as I lay there wondering what I was entitled to.

* * *

Jeff and I walked to a restaurant in the morning. Referring back to the question of what I felt I was entitled to I informed Jeff, "I'm drawing a blank on that one."

"As you should, my friend," he replied.

"At one level I think about things like the United States Constitution and the Bill of Rights but still don't necessarily feel like I'm entitled to what that gives me but I sure am thankful for what it gives me. On a different level, I think about my marriage or being a father to my kids or my education and don't necessarily feel a strong sense of entitlement there either. I guess I expect my education or experience to open some doors for me but it doesn't entitle me to a job. I still have to work to get that and keep it."

The waitress set our food down in front of us and we thanked her. Jeff continued, "If we look at entitlement as a sense that something is owed, a guaranteed benefit, you don't feel the government 'owes' you anything, you don't feel your family 'owes' you anything. How about the other way around? What do you feel you owe them?"

Quickly I said, "That's a big list. We can talk about that for a while. The government does so much for us. We can complain about it all day and point out the ways it doesn't work but when you get down to it, the guys who wrote the constitution created a pretty good system. I mean, we have roads, schools, police, fire departments, libraries, and tons of stuff we just take for granted. We owe a lot to that. I owe my family, even more, they give me so much."

He raised an eyebrow in a questioning look. "So, you owe a lot but are owed little?"

"Well, I don't know. I guess you could say that," I replied unsure if I felt comfortable with the statement. I'm sure I felt owed something but was having a tough time thinking of what.

"Isn't that a lot of Jesus' message? If people lived their lives feeling they owe something instead of feeling they are owed something this world would be a drastically different place. The meek would truly inherit the Earth."

I'd always loved that verse but it sure didn't include me. I wasn't among the meek.

As we finished the simple breakfast of pancakes I looked around the restaurant. This was a lot more comfortable place for me than where we had lunch the day before. Jeff left his usual enormous tip and we headed out.

* * *

Once on the road, well past St. Louis, Jeff picked up my phone to tell Luke we would be there shortly after noon. We chatted about inconsequentials, listened to the radio, or just drove in silence as Jeff read and I watched the landscape alternate between farmland and partially wooded areas.

As the sun rose higher in the sky, the distance between us and HRI was growing fast. I had many mixed emotions but, in the end,

I had to trust, or at least try to trust, Jeff had a reason for me to have a short stay there.

Listening to the radio news there was a story about *The Change*'s most recent concert and what he was doing in that city, bringing groups together to work together. Or, with my Derrick realization, building connections. As I listened I had a profound sense the world was changing. I smiled to myself because it was clear Marcus had chosen a good pseudonym for himself.

Then I found myself dismissing the feeling, rationalizing it. Sure, I was going through a drastic change due to everything I had been through but I shouldn't project that on the rest of the world. Things were changing but things always change. I was seeing things differently and thinking the world was changing but instead it was me changing.

Deep in my reflections, the drive went quickly. We were approaching Kansas City before I knew it and I got excited and nervous at the same time about visiting Luke. The residual fear from the drug house still echoed in my brain.

On the trip here, Jeff and I had many bizarre experiences and met some interesting people. Like everyone we met, Luke never totally left my mind during these last two months. I often wondered what happened after we left him at the church.

We had seen Derrick and we were going to see Sally at her wedding. But I wondered about Bear and Harris? What happened to them after we had met them?

Jeff interrupted my reflections, "You ready for lunch or at least want a drink? I could sure use something."

I looked at my gas gauge; it wasn't as far down as I usually go but figured we could fill up anyway. "Sure, we can get gas too."

We were approaching the outskirts of Kansas City and I pulled into the next exit. As I pulled into the gas station restaurant combo it didn't take me long to realize Jeff had done it again. This was where we had the experience with the goofy mobile.

I pulled up to a pump and started looking around to see if I could figure out why we were here. Jeff and I walked in, he got in line to pay for gas and I went to the attached fast food restaurant and got us some food.

When we came out, I saw what I was looking for pulled up to the pump beside us. The rims that cost more than the car were gone, the out-of-place hood ornament was gone, the continental kits were gone, and the guy pumping gas had two usable hands. An *"Invite The Change"* decal was about the only ornamentation on the car.

Smiling, I looked at Jeff and he gave me a knowing smile back. We got up to the gas pump by my car and although the stereo was on in their car it was down to a polite level, and strangely, I felt like singing along:

> *In the past we had the mega follower.*
> *It won't last, no more lie swallower.*
> *The lie of the image, the lust of the power*
> *Dies like the passage of seeds that won't flower.*

Jeff said to the two guys at the car, "Hey friends, I really like that song."

The passenger calmly looked out his rolled-down window at Jeff. The man pumping gas, the one who threatened Jeff last time, also looked in our direction. There was a moment before he said anything during which his face had an inquisitive look as if he was trying to place Jeff. Last time, Jeff's face was so battered I doubted the man could make the connection.

Meekly the driver replied, "Man, this guy's the best. I quit listening to those other guys."

"Why's that?" inquired Jeff.

The man looked at Jeff strangely again; he was still trying to place Jeff. I watched Jeff's look in return. When I first saw Jeff at the stoplight at the start of my trip, there was something about him that commanded I look at him and once I did, his look was unnervingly calm. As much as I wanted to leave him there, I couldn't. Jeff's look right now seemed to invite the man into safety. Jeff was a safe place to fall.

I started to wish I had that characteristic but then thought of Keith back at HRI. I was the safe place to fall for him. Then Dylan came to mind. I was his safe place to fall. I did have that characteristic. It just didn't ooze out of me as it did with Jeff.

Holding the pump handle in the gas spout the man looked at the gas-stained concrete reflecting on this question with *The Change* playing in the background. He looked at Jeff. "You hear those words? Every time I listen to them they slap me and tell me how stupid I was. Man, I would've worn a shoe on my head like a hat if one of those other guys did that. 'Mega follower.' Exactly what I was."

Jeff looked at him questioningly. "The music makes you feel bad so you listen to it?"

The guy huffed out a laugh. "Sounds dumb when you say it like that. But yeah, it makes me feel bad but also keeps telling me I'm better than how I was living."

He looked up at Jeff intently. There was something he wanted to say and was unsure about continuing. Jeff's gaze invited him to safety and the driver tentatively started. "A couple of months ago, right here at this gas station, I had something strange happen. These two guys at the pump asked me to turn down my music. One looked like he just got the smack beat out of him." He looked back at Jeff, then at me, and back to Jeff. "That's all I remember about 'em. Back then I was too caught up in myself, in my anger to notice much. I was listening to that junk I used to listen to and the guy asked me to change it and when I wouldn't he snapped his fingers and it changed. Then he made my car not work so we were stuck here until he made our car work again."

Jeff calmly said, "Really?"

The driver paused, and then with an anxious look asked the question that was bothering him, "It was you, wasn't it?"

Jeff only nodded.

"You looked pretty bad last time but you act just like him. Who are you?"

Jeff shook his head this time and answered, "That's not important. You're important. Your change is important."

His pump clicked off so the man lifted it out and hung it up. He looked over at me but then solemnly turned back to Jeff. "Change — *The Change* — My Change." He put his gas cap on then turned and leaned against his car. His passenger just leaned against the door's window opening watching without talking.

The driver then looked directly at Jeff. "You're not important? What happened that day, what you did, did something to me. I don't know, it's like I started seeing things different, like I walked out of a fog, like a different part of my brain started working. Soon after that, *The Change* started being played out here. That part of my brain started working."

That statement struck me. The last time we were here Jeff said something about using our modern brain to drive us forward.

The new modern brain man continued, "I spent a lot of time thinking after that. Things were no longer right but I didn't know what direction was right." He looked back at his passenger. "The others quit hanging with me 'cept him. He's the only one that even seemed close to understanding. Then I watched the fights for *The Change's* release party just like everybody did and as I watched how he handled himself, I realized he was different. His power was not about him." He softly laughed to himself, "I'm not even sure what that means but that's the only way I can describe it. Nothing he did seemed 'bout him. I mean, even the title of his album, *It's Not About Me*, wasn't just a title, it's the truth. I started listening more to *The Change* and what he said made sense. I mean, 'Mega follower' really made sense. All of those other guys are just bringing us down, not helping us."

I was surprised how much of his 'hood' dialect was gone. Unlike last time, he was sounding like a reasonably intelligent person. He went on, "Lost lots of friends since then. That's okay though. Not even sure they were friends. Most of those other rappers have made us look like fools for a long time and even worse, we gave them the power to do it."

Jeff responded, "Wow, that's some statement."

"Not a good one." He looked deep in thought with that. "You have someone like Martin Luther King who did so much for us and then you get guys like that who let us take it away from ourselves. It's no good."

"What's your name, friend?" asked Jeff.

"Deon," the driver replied.

I was simply blown away. Jeff had asked the other guys drinking beer by their car about *The Change*. They said they liked *The Change* yet they didn't seem to understand what the message was. Now, this guy was profoundly taken by the message.

Jeff said, "Well Deon, you know *The Change* is playing near here pretty soon."

Deon grinned. "Yeah, looking forward to that. Maybe it'll help move things."

Jeff offered, "I have backstage passes if you want. I can even arrange for you and your friend to spend some time with him the day before if you're interested. He likes to get a tour of the area before the concert to get a feel for the community."

"What? You can do that?" the driver asked in amazement.

"For the right people, I can." Jeff went to the back passenger door and pulled the passes out of his backpack. "And you seem like the right people. Show him some of the things happening here to rebuild the community or take him to some places that need to get things happening to rebuild the community. He can make things happen."

His passenger got out of the car now, eager to see the passes.

Deon exclaimed, "This's great! Some stuff is happening but not much. Havin' him come here will get people excited."

"Give me your phone, Deon." Unquestioningly the driver handed it to Jeff and Jeff dialed. "Marcus? I got you some people willing to show you around before your KC concert."

I guess he wasn't worried about Deon having Marcus's personal number.

Jeff listened to Marcus's reply and then followed up, "I thought you'd like that. Here they are." Jeff passed the phone back to Deon who took it as if he was an archeologist being handed an ancient artifact. Deon spoke into the phone as Jeff and I waved goodbye, got in our car, and headed back out.

I slowed for a speed bump and my mind drifted back a couple of months. "Last time we were here you used a chair metaphor. You said Deon had plenty of people pulling him off the chair but he needed someone strong enough to pull him up on the chair and keep him there. You've been planning *The Change* thing for a while."

He turned and gave me a soft punch in the shoulder. "Would you believe it was a lucky guess?"

I laughed and jokingly added, "It must have been. It's the only logical explanation."

As we pulled out of the station, I replayed the events in my mind. "Why were these guys so affected by *The Change* but the guys drinking beer in the slums of Chicago seemed to have no real appreciation for Marcus's message?"

"You expect everybody, all over, to change instantly because of a really good message? You expecting a miracle?" Jeff roared with laughter.

I couldn't help but laugh either. It was pretty funny coming from Jeff. After he quit laughing he said, "Change happens at its own pace and in its own place, when and where it's ready to happen. It will reach those guys too, and when it does it may or may not be a drastic change like we saw with Deon and his friend. I doubt the guys drinking by the car will read the book but the movie may have a bigger impact on them."

"What book? What movie?" I asked.

"Come on Stanley, we've already talked about that. *The Change* is only part of the plan for getting the message out."

"Oh yeah, I forgot about that. When are you going to finish writing the book? I haven't heard you talk about it for a while." That was a book and movie I wanted to read and watch.

He looked at me like I was crazy. "I'm not writing it. I got someone else doing it. Like everything else with this change, it'll happen when it's ready to happen."

I looked at him with a slightly annoyed look, then jokingly said, "Aw, so it may not be out for Christmas. Guess I won't put that on my Christmas wish list. So, what's this book/movie going to be about? Like an update to the Bible? I can't see a movie being done on something like that."

He shook his head, "No, nothing like that. It's going to be a story. Remember, I'm not writing it, but I see it being about a couple that's going through a tough time but, because of their love for each other, they make it through with wonderful grace. You know, grow and mature together."

I looked at him with raised eyebrows. "A love story? You have to be kidding me? Your plan is to change the world with a chick flick?"

He looked at me confused. "What? That's not a good idea? It's a touching story, friend."

I knew his look of confusion was just part of his playing with me. If he is a messiah out to change the world, he was a very cool one. "No, that's a really stupid idea."

He rubbed his chin as if he was thinking hard. "Hmmm, not a chick flick. Let's see. What if I kept the whole couple in love thing and added a couple of good fight scenes and a car chase?"

"The couple fighting?"

He shook his head in total disagreement. "No, no, no. Real fight scenes with blood and everything."

Now I rubbed my chin as if deep in thought. "Hmmm, maybe. If it's done right, that might work. If the chase scene ends with a fiery crash, maybe."

Jeff slowly brought his hand across in front of him. "I was envisioning the chase ending with a car crashing into a swimming pool."

I nodded. "That would be cool." I picked up my phone and offered it to him. "You better call and tell your writer the new ideas. Is this another thing Marcus is doing?"

He didn't take the phone. "No, Marcus would be good, but he's too busy. I have another guy doing it that's pretty good. He'll work those changes in without a problem." He rubbed his chin again. "I like those changes. That'll open it up to a wider audience. Good ideas, Stanley. I'm glad we talked."

What a character. "No problem. Glad I can at least save the world from one more chick flick or romance novel."

Chapter 52

As the mile markers passed by I kept thinking about Deon. Even with his about-face, there was a sadness to him that was bothering me. After rolling that around in my mind I commented to Jeff, "You know, for a guy that seems to have a future in front of him, there's a sadness to Deon."

He put down his book and got a thoughtful look. "That's pretty observant, Stanley. I'm glad you noticed because it's something you need to think about."

I looked at him confused, "How so?"

"Deon's starting his vertical growth. But as beautiful and altruistic as it sounds, it's rarely a pleasant journey and often it's a lonely journey. Deon's discovering that."

I thought of Deon saying some of his previous companions wouldn't hang out with him anymore. What would that mean for me? I got kind of worried. I said the first people who came to mind, "Beth? My kids?" I gave Jeff a panicked look. Beth and I are polar opposites in many ways. She'd been surprisingly supportive throughout this but I had a feeling my vertical growth might take me in directions that would strain our relationship and therefore strain the relationship with my kids.

Jeff looked at me as if he was actually thinking about what direction to go with his answer. If I didn't know him better, I would say he was running different conversations through his mind to see how they sounded there before he let them out of his mouth. But, I thought, Jeff doesn't do that. Jeff always knows what to say. He knows how things work out in the future. I felt my heart starting to beat harder and my hands tensed on the steering wheel.

My voice was shaky. "Jeff? You see the future. You know what happens. Do I lose my family?"

Slowly he opened his mouth but paused before speaking. "I see many futures, Stanley. Each action takes the future in one direction or another. Your question, your fear, my answer, this moment, create a future. My friend, as much as I love you and care for you, you have to trust me that answering this question is not something I should do."

The car next to me honked as I drifted into their lane. I touched the brake to turn off the cruise control and then watched the mirrors as I made my way to the shoulder and stopped.

"Beth and I don't make it through this?"

His eyes narrowed and produced as much of a worried look as I had ever seen on his face. "I didn't say that."

I tried to smile. "So, we are okay? We grow together?"

His lips grew thin. "I didn't say that either, Stanley." He paused as he thought more about what to say. "In the path I'm steering towards, things work out for you and things work out for Beth. But me telling you what that means changes the future and the chances of things working out for the two of you goes down."

I had my hands on the steering wheel and looked straight in front of me as cars zoomed by. This was unlike Jeff. He always knew what to say and how to say it. Why was he doing this now? The blog article I wrote just before the craziness with Jeff came to mind. In it, I had said there are three logical places to find meaning in life, religion, work, and family. This trip with Jeff had started giving me meaning in religion, maybe spirituality was a better word. At HRI I started finding meaning in work. Was I going to trade those for meaning in my family? If so, that wasn't a fair trade. Vertical growth may not be what it's cracked up to be.

I brought my head slowly forward to the steering wheel. "Can you tell me if Beth and the kids will be happy? I mean, with what I'm doing, what I'm going through, will I make their lives unhappy?"

I heard a sigh beside me and imagined his face with the same uneasy look. "There will be difficult times, times where there will not be happiness. Those are times of growth. Don't minimize the need for those times. But in the end, all of you will be better off and happier."

I rotated my head to look at him but left it on the steering wheel. "Not sure if that makes it any better."

Jeff nodded in understanding but said nothing.

I felt like I should say more, ask more questions but nothing was coming to mind. With effort, I put my back against the seat, checked my driver's side mirror, and pulled back on the road. We drove in an uncomfortable silence for a long time.

* * *

"Take the exit for the church where we dropped Luke off."

I didn't respond but took the exit. Then I tried to remember as much about Luke as I could. I remembered how intimidating he was when Jeff and I saw him alongside the road with the flat tire. He was a big, scary-looking young man and Jeff took no notice of that. Luke's persona broke down later at the drug house though.

Luckily, I didn't have to deal with the reflection long because soon Jeff directed me off the highway and through a vaguely familiar town until we pulled in front of an unfamiliar building at the end of a row of unfamiliar buildings. Just two months earlier, there was a shabby church housed in an old, abandoned store, connected to a row of abandoned, graffiti-covered, retail buildings. Those buildings were no longer abandoned. The church was no longer shabby. We watched a group of kids walk into the freshly painted building next to the church. There was a sign above it that read, "Youth Center." Potted plants, in full bloom, lined the row of buildings. There was a thrift store, a grocery store, and a library, all fully renovated with people walking in and out of them.

I got out of the car and stared. "How much money was in that wad you gave the Reverend?" I looked at Jeff and pointed at the church. "Almost every window in that building was covered with plywood and now it looks like the latest trend in modern design."

"Let's ask Luke and the Reverend." Jeff motioned for me to go to the church.

We walked up to the new doors for the building and above them was an impressively artistic sign saying, *"Church of Undying Love."* On both windows on either side of the door were large decals with *"Invite The Change."* We walked into a bright fellowship area. Last time, with all the windows boarded up, the area had been dark and dingy. It seemed like a different building now.

I took my focus off the building as I looked at the person sitting on the altar railing, it was Luke. He looked up and the three people sitting on the front pew facing him turned towards us. I recognized the humble-looking minister from our last visit here. A man and woman, looking to be in their mid-50's turned back towards Luke. When Luke smiled and stood, the man and woman got up and hurried back towards us.

The speed they came at us scared me at first. I was wondering why these people would want to attack us but as soon as they got there they were both crying uncontrollably and I found myself fiercely embraced by this sobbing female stranger, not quite sure where to put my hands or what I should do. I looked to Jeff for guidance but he had his arms around the man and was facing the other direction. I followed his example and put my arms around her.

Luke and the minister followed at a more peaceful pace. They both had beautiful smiles of happiness and gave Jeff and me embraces while the man and woman were still holding us and crying.

It was an uncomfortably long time before she released me. The man released Jeff but kept one hand on Jeff's shoulders and wiped the tears away with the other. The man looked towards me and then back to Jeff. "I can never pay you two back for giving Monica and me our son back. We'll always be indebted to you two," the man said through tears and a broken voice.

Luke said, "Let me introduce my parents, Fred and Monica."

It now made sense who these people were. I remembered what Jeff said to Luke on the highway about throwing his parent's love back in their faces.

"You owe nothing more than you ever owed and what you owe is not to Stanley nor me," Jeff said in reply.

I wished Jeff did not include me. The only thing I did that day was panic.

"We got our son back! Fred and I are forever indebted!" said Monica.

Jeff looked over at Luke, smiling deeply at him. "Luke, my friend, how about this world that doesn't give a 'darn'?"

This brought back the image of Luke when we first met him. He was dressed to play the role of a thug, and Jeff was referencing the quote on Luke's Marilyn Manson T-shirt he wore that day.

Luke still had the bandana holding back his long brown hair and dressed in worn jeans and a T-shirt but he presented himself much better today than he did two months ago.

Luke's response to Jeff contained a smile that was a cross between one of knowing an answer and one of grateful humility. "I was greatly mistaken. You've given me more than you've even given my parents. You've given me my parents back and my life back. And I have a purpose."

It was strange listening to Luke. His voice was different in a way I couldn't describe. It didn't have the angry, condescending tone he had on the highway, but it was more than that. It had a sense of knowledge, of understanding, of peace. It was a voice that caused you to listen when he spoke. It was a striking difference, very striking.

Luke turned and put his arm around the humble old man and brought him forward. "Reverend Smith runs this church and runs a prison ministry. He's taken this broken soul under his wing and is teaching me what I should've learned when my parents were trying to teach me."

Reverend Smith beamed, not with pride, but with happiness. You could see in his eyes this man rarely thought of himself. He was happy Luke found his way and Luke's parents had their son.

Looking at Luke, I said, "You look good. Looks like you've been getting some sun."

He let out a soulful laugh. "Yeah, hanging out in drug houses at night and sleeping during the day tends to give a person a bit of a vampire complexion. Spent the last two months in the sun with paintbrushes, hammers, and saws in my hand during the day and the Bible in my hand at night." He held up a bandaged hand. "Seems there's a bit of a learning curve with saws."

His comment about the Bible let me know Jeff was right two months ago about Luke finding a book to read in the church. I looked around. "Looks like you're tackling that learning curve pretty fast."

He looked around. "It's not me. I mean, sure, I've been helping but we contacted that *Invite The Change* group and they've been like piranhas."

The Reverend put his hand on Luke's arm and smiled warmly. "I don't like that analogy, Luke. It makes them sound bad. Like we've been attacked. It is quite different. Quite different than anything we've ever had before. I've been here for over fifty years and have seen many good-willed people come in to try to help. They came in and told us what we need. When I was young, I listened, because I figured they knew what this community needed better than an inexperienced young man. But what happened every time is that they got the programs started and then left. Without them, the programs dwindled and died, leaving a hole in our community. I don't blame them. They were good-hearted people. It's just that they didn't understand the community and what the community needed."

Luke held up his hand. "Okay, not piranhas. I'll try to come up with a better visual." He looked at us. "But some people from that group came in and the first thing they did was start walking around and talking to people. Then they started going to surrounding communities and talking to other churches and businesses. They went to the schools and started talking. After a week of this, they asked me and the Rev to invite people to a meeting. Before the meeting, they talked to us about what they learned about the community and gave some ideas. When the meeting came around, there was a video camera set up, and they were nowhere to be seen."

With a strange look, I said, "That doesn't sound good."

Luke went on. "Yeah, that's what I thought but what happened was, the Rev and I started talking about what was needed and once the people started talking, they couldn't shut up. They said the kids need something to do to keep them out of trouble. They said they couldn't get to the grocery stores because they didn't have cars, so they did their shopping at the convenience stores. They talked on and on. The day after the meeting, the *Invite The Change* people came back. We got some of the local leaders together from the schools, churches, and businesses. We got some of the active local residents in here and we all watched that video. We watched it over and over. We talked about ideas and what it would take to do them. The Rev said he would like to open a youth center and the building next door was just sitting empty. The next week a different guy walks in with a title for all the buildings on this block owned by a non-profit they created with me and the Rev as the directors. There was a fund attached to it to cover the taxes for the foreseeable future."

Reverend Smith interrupted. "They gave us money to hire some of the homeless and unemployed people around here to remodel the buildings." He smiled excitedly. "Do you see the difference? We invited the change in, but it was our change. It was what we created. This community designed the change. The people who came in were our helpers, not our saviors. If they stop coming, the community still has all of this. The community needs the grocery store and it's owned by a wonderful local couple thanks to a low-cost loan. They rent it from the non-profit. Luke and I set the rent amount. The thrift store is a thriving business owned by three local women who brought us a business proposal. Luke and I, as directors of the non-profit, were able to help them get funding, training, and start the business. They have a staff of ten people now, who walk no more than two blocks to work. These were unemployed people just two months ago. This is our community's grocery store, our community's thrift store, our community's youth center, our community's library. If *Invite The Change* folds up and ends tomorrow, we still have something the community needs. It's ours."

When Reverend Smith said, 'not our saviors', it reminded me of my conversation with Marcus when I first met him at HRI. Marcus talked about Jeff coming in to 'rescue' Marcus and he didn't want any part of it. "Yeah, I see the difference. It's the community asking for help, inviting change, but being an active part in that change. I can see where that would inspire people in the community." I looked around. "And you guys have done so much since we were here last."

Luke started to talk but stopped. He paused while looking at Jeff as his expression became a mixture of awe and confusion. "Your timing that day was amazing, Jeff. When you led me through that door," he pointed at the entrance, "two months ago, Reverend Smith was at the altar praying for the future of this church, the community, and the prison ministry." Luke watched Jeff to see how he responded.

Jeff simply looked curious for Luke to continue.

Luke slowly started back up. "You see, Reverend Smith doesn't have much time left. He is terminally ill and there's no one to take over his ministry. That prayer was interrupted when you led me through the door."

I felt like adding a sarcastic, "Imagine that," but refrained. Instead, I just exchanged a quick smile with Jeff.

Luke positioned himself between his parents and put his arms around them. "It's funny, I'm part of a prison ministry now. Two months ago my future was leading me to jail and now, it's still leading me to jail, but on the right side of the bars. I'm making a difference here and in the jail. And believe it or not, I'm starting seminary next semester."

I watched Fred and Monica's faces light up with this. From their perspective, they must have witnessed a miraculous change in Luke. Even from my perspective, it looked that way.

Jeff said, "That's great, Luke. Let's go see what you and the Reverend have happening at the jail."

Luke smiled. "I'd love to but it isn't that easy. Security is very tight out there. They have to run background checks and such. Otherwise, I'd love to show you."

Jeff nodded his head back and forth. "Stanley and I already have clearance there. We can get in without an issue."

Luke looked at Jeff with a brain full of questions in his eyes. I knew his questions but my experience with Jeff let me just leave them alone. They weren't the ones I wanted answered. Luke, showing he was a faster learner than me, decided to forgo asking the questions and looked at his parents. "Do you guys mind? I mean, I hate leaving you but …"

"Why not bring them?" Jeff asked.

"They haven't been out there with me yet. We need to get them approved."

Monica smiled politely. "Sweetie, it's okay. Maybe we can come some other time. We would love to see what you're doing."

Jeff nonchalantly answered, "They have clearance, too."

Monica said, "No, we haven't done that. But it's okay, you guys go."

The smile Luke gave showed humored awe as he looked at Jeff. "Mom, I watched him pull the trigger of a loaded gun pointed at his head. We walked out of a house during a police raid without even being questioned. I think you guys have what you need to join us." She was about to question him but Luke spoke first. "Stanley, you just want to follow us out there?"

This whole time Reverend Smith had been standing quietly just staring at Jeff. Now, slowly he shuffled his feet forward up to Jeff, took Jeff's hand, knelt before him, and looked at the ground. "Thank you," was all his meek voice uttered.

Jeff helped the frail man to his feet and said, "You've done great work in your life and it will continue and grow because of your faith. You are a blessed man."

A gentle smile came to Reverend Smith's face and his eyes widened. "Yes, I've lived a blessed life and now that I've been blessed with Luke, I can die with peace."

It was interesting the way he talked about his death with such great happiness.

The old man turned to Luke with a loving smile. "I only hope I can live long enough to see him finish seminary."

Luke said, "I hope so, too."

We were all quiet for a moment until Jeff finally spoke. "You ready to take us to the prison? I'm looking forward to seeing what you're doing."

"More than ready," replied Luke excitedly. He looked at his mom and dad. "You can ride with the rev and me."

Chapter 53

Jeff and I got in the Jetta and followed Luke's car through the streets of Kansas City and out of town for about twenty or thirty minutes. The sight of tall fences lined with razor wire as we drove into the parking lot didn't bring me any excitement about my latest escapade with Jeff. We pulled up beside Luke's car as they got out.

Fred and Monica surveyed the surroundings with the same apprehensive face I'm sure I had. Fred said, "Never been to a jail before." He looked at Monica. "Now that I'm here I kind of wonder why it never occurred to me before."

Monica continued his thought. "Seems like we could have done something to help. Not sure what, but something."

I watched them as they looked around studying the surroundings. I couldn't help but wonder why a couple as good as they appeared had a son like the one Jeff and I met on the highway that day.

Luke's voice turned my attention to him. "Believe me, there are ways you two can help if you want. But let's get in there. Just leave everything in the cars except for your driver's license and car keys. That makes getting through security easier."

Jeff opened his door and threw a folded stack of money into the floor in front of his seat and then pulled his driver's license from his back pocket and looked at it. I pulled my license from my wallet and put that in the center console. Then I emptied the change, pocket knife, and other contents of my pocket there also. I removed all the keys from the fob and dropped them in with a ka-ching as they hit the change. As I started backing out of the car I looked at the hundred-dollar bill wrapped around what I assumed was other hundred-dollar bills. Jeff, cash, driver's license, books, and a small backpack for a cross-country trip. For as complex of a person as he was also very simple.

At the door to the prison, Luke pressed a buzzer and a crackly voice of a man came over the speaker at the door inquiring about our business there.

"Prison ministry, this is Luke and Reverend Smith with some guests."

"Just a minute," the crackly voice requested.

We all waited quietly but I don't think it was a full minute before a female voice came over the speaker. "They're just assembling in the chapel now. They should be ready for all of you by the time we get checked in but I'll speed that along." There was a click of the magnetic lock releasing the door.

Luke gave Reverend Smith a confused look. "Assembling? Ready for us? Did you tell them we were coming?"

The old man shook his head. "No, I haven't called the prison since you started helping me. So, I don't know."

Luke looked at the other four of us apologetically. "Sorry, I don't know what they mean. Usually, we just go meet with some of the men at the chapel or the visitor area." He grabbed the handle and opened the door for us.

A tall, thin, uniformed woman exited a door, entered the hallway, and came our way. The clicking of her boots hitting the concrete floors and the jingle of her keys echoed in against the light gray cinder block walls. I felt like I should be nervous about this whole jail situation, and was up to this point, but her smile, as she approached us, offset that feeling. When she got to us she set a stack of clipboards on a table and held a metal detector wand up. She started talking quickly, "Hello Luke and Reverend Smith." They tried to greet her back but she didn't wait. "People are excited so let's get this going. I just need all of you to sign those after I wand you and see your IDs. Everything's been filled out. Just empty your pockets into the baskets on the table."

Within a few minutes, she had all of us cleared to enter and quickly turned and beckoned us to follow. Again, the sound of her boots and the jingle of the keys bounced off the walls with nothing to deaden the sound. I wanted to ask what was happening but was instead focused on keeping up with this woman. I looked at the

Reverend and saw his look of confusion but his mental effort was even more focused on keeping up with her.

We had two short breaks as the guard used her keys to slide open the light green metal bar door and then shut it with an eerie final thud both times. I tried to imagine what the sound meant to prisoners. Once you heard it you know the only direction was straight ahead to the prison. Thankfully we had a free pass to the other direction today, but there was a finality to the sound, nevertheless.

Finally, the guard stopped at a door marked with a small sign denoting it was the chapel. "We're here and you have a crowd waiting. Thank you for doing this. It's exciting."

Reverend Smith looked at her to question but Jeff put his arm over the man's shoulder and led him through the door.

I should have felt sorry for the Reverend but instead felt a guilty joy seeing I wasn't the only victim of Jeff's mental games. I followed them through the door. I wasn't sure what I expected to see but this wasn't it. There must have been over fifty men in orange prison suits seated with their backs to us in dozen rows of pews divided by a center aisle, and about ten guards either standing against the two-tone tan and brown windowless chapel walls or happily chatting with one of the men in orange.

In the back corner, about fifteen feet to the left of us, with a scowl on his face as he watched the six of us walk in, was an impressively tall and broad-shouldered black man in a suit and tie, leaning against the wall with his arms crossed. My eyes met his and I felt my knees start to shake so I looked away. The mood of the room was happy and excited, but this man seemed to be removed from that atmosphere.

Jeff gave both Luke and Reverend Smith a polite shove to get them walking forward down the center aisle. Luke's parents and I followed the three of them. I expected to hear our tour guide's boots behind us hitting the gray concrete floor but when I didn't I turned and saw she stayed at the door smiling. I glanced at the man in the suit. He wasn't smiling as he focused on us making our way to the front of the chapel.

Once Luke and the Reverend were beside the inmates, the greetings started. Reverend Smith addressed every man he greeted by name. The ones he couldn't hug or reach with his hand, he waved at.

One man said, "Word spread ya have some good news. What's happening?"

Somewhat embarrassed the old man shrugged and said, "I don't know." He turned to Luke who was also greeting the men. "What is happening? Why all of this?"

Luke scanned the room and then looked at Jeff and me. "Not sure but I guess we'll be finding out."

Once at the front of the room, Jeff whispered in the Reverend's ear. He looked at Jeff questioningly and whispered back. Jeff nodded and gave him a gentle nudge toward the podium. Jeff then joined the four of us against the wall to the far left of the podium. The eyes of the man in the suit in the adjacent corner watched as Reverend Smith slowly took his place in front of the room and they quieted without any prompting. A gentle, frail voice addressed them. "This room is filled with some of the dearest friends I've ever had. All of you have blessed my life and I'm overjoyed seeing so many of you all here at once. This is a truly special moment for me. Two months ago, I had a prayer fully answered. As you know, we have been blessed with Luke as an answer to that prayer."

There was a rustle of agreement from the men listening. It was evident Reverend Smith was loved here and Luke was building off that bond.

The rustle died down and the Reverend gently continued. "I don't pretend to have many answers. The only thing I'm certain of is love, compassion, and acceptance are so very, very important. I have watched that flower blossom in so many of you and the power which surges through me each time I'm here makes it hard for this old man to sleep at night. I want to dance but my body says no, so my mind dances with joy."

A chuckle passed through the crowd and I understood why. From my short time with him, this sentence brought a very interesting image of him dancing. It also brought a sense of respect.

He continued, "I've spent my life learning to love truer and trying to plant that seed in others. My one true belief is, I believe in love. My dearest friends, today I have met love incarnate. I would be honored if he would let you see it too." He turned to Jeff with a hopeful smile.

The words, "love incarnate" caught me. I looked over at Jeff and, for the first time ever; I saw reluctance on his face. I recalled questioning him one Sunday about not preaching. He said that wasn't his place. And it was true. Even at HRI, he was mostly behind the scenes.

As he slowly came forward, "love incarnate" became the perfect words to describe Jeff. He was the cause of the most stressful parts of my life, but looking back, it was so easy to see every action had been taken from a place of pure love for me, to teach me and help me grow. Every action he took with everyone was pure and profound love. Jeff was indeed, "love incarnate."

Jeff stood there smiling and scanning the audience, a congregation of people deemed not worthy to live with the rest of society. His smile and eyes radiated love and peace, and the crowd was transfixed on an internal beauty that shined through the fairly normal exterior.

I wondered and looked towards Reverend Smith as he beamed towards Jeff in awe. He had knelt before Jeff at the church. Did he see Jeff for what Jeff truly was? A bit of jealousy took hold within me. As badly as I wanted to, I'm still not sure I see Jeff for what he is. Maybe I was too close or still held too many doubts. "Love incarnate." Words from a special man to describe a special man.

In contrast, I saw the man in the suit slowly take about five steps forward from the wall to focus on Jeff more intently. He stood between the left wall and pews with his head cocked to the side as he studied Jeff with the ever-present scowl.

Jeff started slowly. "From what I see today, the love of one man is doing great work." Jeff turned and gave Reverend Smith a look of gratitude.

He then stepped away from the podium with a thoughtful look, put his hands in his pockets, and took a few paces as he looked down towards the ground. He then turned and paced back, looked up, and examined the audience.

Fred leaned over to me. "When Luke told me about this guy, I tried to imagine the man who could finally break through to my son. Luke always had so much potential but gravitated to the bad. Fought us incessantly." Fred looked up at Jeff. "But I look at him and see something. Not sure what, but something."

I turned from Fred to Jeff. Yes, he is something, I thought. From my perspective to the far left of the pulpit, I watched Jeff and he seemed uncomfortable as he waited for the right words. The room was drawn into him as they waited.

"I love what Reverend Smith said. 'Love, compassion, and acceptance, are so very, very important.' I'm especially glad he added acceptance. Love and compassion both get attention but acceptance is the forgotten cousin. Yet, acceptance is the most powerful sign of love. You only have to look to Reverend Smith to see what I mean."

Jeff looked out into the filled pews, the guards standing along the wall, and the man in the suit. "Look at the men around you. If you ask any of them their story, there will be a story of rejection. The characters in their story may include parents, neighbors, teachers, siblings, classmates and the list goes on. If you ask them to tell their story, there will also be characters who offered acceptance." Jeff held out his hand as if he was offering something. "If you drink this, I will accept you. If you smoke this, I will accept you. If you take that old lady's money, I will accept you. If you rob that store, I will accept you."

Jeff paused again as the faces in the chapel absorbed his words. "But if you look at why you are here in this room today at this moment, it's a pure and beautiful form of acceptance. I watched Reverend Smith as we walked in today. He has accepted each and every one of you for who you are at this moment, with no conditions. That acceptance is the foundation for growth but growth is not a condition for that acceptance. Acceptance is a basic need, and until that need is fulfilled, we can't grow."

My mind pictured Derrick, Jeff, and me talking at the gas station's restaurant. The word which came out of that experience was "connections." Here the word was "acceptance." They were two aspects of the same thing. I was accepted by Jeff the moment we met. I was accepted at HRI the moment I walked in. I was privileged to watch how that acceptance transformed Keith, the convenience store worker who Grace got a job at HRI. He was accepted for who he was at the place he was in his life, without any conditions. He was never asked to change, but because of that acceptance, change happened and he connected with HRI and its people at a deep level.

Neural pathways were reforming in my head as Jeff spoke. He never asked me to change but his unconditional acceptance allowed me to connect with him at a profound level which wouldn't allow me to stay the same.

Acceptance and connection became words with a fuller meaning to me but I sensed a hole that needed to be filled. I turned my attention back to Jeff hoping he would give me the words to fill the hole.

Jeff raised his right arm in front of him and moved it from right to left as if he was drawing everyone in. "Now that you've seen what acceptance looks like, look at the people next to you. Can you follow the model Reverend Smith has shown? Can you accept others unconditionally?" Jeff let the question set as the men looked around. He calmly shrugged. "To be honest, that seems like too much. What Reverend Smith models has taken a lifetime to perfect, so start small. Pick one or two people and work on accepting them without conditions. Once you can do that, add another person. Once you get the hang of it there is one person I want you to add. He will be the most difficult person to accept unconditionally. But you will go nowhere until you've accepted him. I ask you to add yourself to that list."

I smiled. That was the hole. I needed to learn to accept myself. I needed to learn to connect with myself. The words acceptance and connection were complete but the work only started two months ago. I had a lot of practice ahead of me as I continue my vertical growth.

Jeff went on. "But please don't confuse self-acceptance with ego. A big ego is a strong sign of little self-acceptance."

Or too little of an ego, I thought. I wasn't fighting off an overly active ego.

"With your journey of growth in mind, I want you to think about something." Jeff paused, looked around, and smiled with a humorous thought in his head. "Each of you here has something the outside world doesn't. The state has given you something many others don't have. Does anyone know what that is?"

It was assumed to be a rhetorical question because no one answered. They were all engrossed in what Jeff was saying. It was interesting watching him. He wasn't preaching to the group and he wasn't speaking to them. It was more like he was having a conversation with each individual in the room.

Jeff answered matter-of-factly. "The state has given you time. You are serving time. You are a servant of time. Now..." He held up his hands beside him and cocked his head. "... how will you serve time? You have a couple of choices and they are your choices to make. I accept you for who you are. Reverend Smith and Luke accept you for who you are. So, you can carry on the path you are going on if that path meets your needs. Or, you can serve time by growing. Reverend Smith, Luke, and I will work with the state to turn this facility from an institution of punishment to an institution of change. If you want, with your help, the Department of Corrections will actually start earning its name back. When you join society again you will have an education, you will have a degree, you will have skills and you will have a future."

This produced a cheer from the men in orange as some in the pews stood. The rest of the time, while Jeff spoke, they had quietly absorbed what Jeff was saying. Now there was more noise coming from the crowd as they exchanged comments back and forth.

Jeff waved for Luke and Reverend Smith to come up. Over the noise of the crowd, Jeff said, "I want you to work with Reverend Smith and Luke to be part of this change." As Luke and Reverend Smith came up with Jeff, he motioned for the men to quiet down. Once it was quiet Jeff started again. "We are all part of this change. Now I wanted to let all of you in on a surprise. I haven't told the Reverend or Luke so this is a surprise to them also. *Invite The Change* has taken a special look at this prison and sees a lot of potential to do something different. They have been working with the Warden and prison administration to bring in some programs to create opportunities for all of you." There was a decent size cheer at this. "But, also, *Invite The Change* has made arrangements with the prison to get *The Change* to do a concert right here at the prison." This was followed by a loud cheer.

Both Luke and Reverend Smith looked at me. Luke mouthed, *"The Change?* Here?"

As normal, I was hopelessly uninformed of Jeff's plans. I walked up closer so I could talk over the noise. "He hasn't told me but that isn't a surprise." I figured Jeff didn't want the depth of his relationship with Marcus and involvement with *Invite The Change* known so I downplayed it. "Jeff has a connection with the organization so if he says it is happening, it is happening."

Reverend Smith got excited. "Oh, I just love his music. It is so inspirational. How very exciting."

The excitement was so high that the noise level made it impossible for Jeff to continue addressing the men so Luke, the Reverend, and Jeff went out and talked with the men individually while Monica, Fred, and I stayed against the wall at the front of the room and watched.

Monica leaned over to me and in an awestruck voice said, "He's amazing. To turn Luke around as he did and now do the same with all of these men."

My attention turned to her and Fred. I'd seen what Jeff could do and I was still amazed by him. For these people to be seeing it for the first time must be overwhelming. I smiled and nodded my head in agreement. "Yeah." I was going to add more but out of the corner of my eye, the man in the suit was walking forward and looking directly at us.

Reverend Smith came over in front of us as the man approached. The Reverend was smiling but the man did not smile back. Over the noise in the room, the Reverend said, "Hello, Warden." Then he turned to us, "This is Kent Kenton, the Warden. We go back a long way."

I held out my hand to introduce myself but he just looked at me and bluntly said, "Get your friends. Come to my office." He turned and made his way through the crowd of orange and stood next to the back door.

Reverend Smith smiled as he watched the Warden walk away. "Don't let his gruffness fool you. I've worked with him at this prison for close to thirty years and consider him one of my closest friends. He cares deeply about this place but feels he is fighting a losing battle."

Quickly, I scanned the room for Jeff and waved him towards us. He got Luke's attention and they headed in our direction.

* * *

The Warden's office didn't strike me as a huge step above the rest of the prison. The room was of a good size but painted a cream color, following the same drab colors found throughout the facility. He sat behind a large gray metal utilitarian desk covered in neatly piled stacks of papers as he motioned for Jeff, Luke, and the Reverend to sit in the three brown metal folding chairs he set in front of the desk before he sat down. He looked at me and Luke's parents and sternly asked, "You part of this discussion or just passengers?"

I looked at Fred and Monica hoping they had a better response but they just stared wide-eyed. Taking a breath, I smiled and said, "Mostly passengers, I guess."

He pointed to the couch in the corner behind us. "Sit there! Not much to look at but nice and cushy."

We turned towards the couch. It had seen better days. The ends of the armrests were worn through the red, black, tan, and white plaid fabric with the foam showing. I had to admit, it was the most colorful thing I had seen in the prison yet. The three of us sat with Fred and me at the ends and Monica in the middle. The Warden wasn't wrong, it was cushy.

Kent Kenton's eyes glared at Luke, then moved to Reverend Smith, Jeff, and then over to Luke's parents and me on the couch. A shiver went down my spine as his gaze landed on me.

His voice boomed, "So! What do you expect me to do?" With the scowl on his face, he was not one the lady's bible class would invite to speak to them.

"In what regards?" asked Jeff.

I think Jeff asked more for our benefit than his. It was hard to read the Warden. I couldn't figure out if he was angry with us or just didn't know how to smile.

"Look," he said strongly as he stood, placing his hands on his desk and leaning towards the men facing him, "I've been running this place for twenty-seven years and seen the lowest of low come in here. The things that I have nightmares about are the ones that walk out the front gate after 'paying their debt to society'. Almost every case, the men who walk out those gates are worse than the ones who came through those same gates to be rehabilitated. We let this trash back out into the streets only to do more harm to good people."

The guy did more than make me nervous, I was downright scared. There was only anger in his voice without a hint of warmth or humanity.

Jeff sat listening to him as relaxed and calm as ever, with the same smile of warmth always present on his face. Luke and Reverend Smith sat listening intently, both with relaxed smiles.

The Warden continued. "The only saving grace is that man sitting right there." He pointed a harsh finger at Reverend Smith. "Because of that man, some of the trash that walks in here actually walks out as real men. Then he brought that man in here." He moved his harsh finger to Luke. "And the chapel starts filling up. So, I want to know what you need from me to have real men walk out of here instead of trash."

I still had problems understanding this guy. He sounded so angry, so cold, yet what he wanted was not to put criminals back out on the street.

Jeff started to talk but the Warden held up his finger to stop him. He thumbed through some papers on his desk and then pulled some out. "*The Change.* Some organization called *Invite The Change.*" He looked at Jeff. "And you're part of all of this, right?"

Jeff nodded.

Kenton looked at the papers again. "Got this two weeks ago. Says, Jeff Havens will be here today to represent the organization, announce the concert and here you are."

Jeff smiled warmly at him. "Thanks for allowing the concert here."

Kenton laid the papers back on the pile. "Signed those and had them sent back thirty seconds after I got them. I watched that big deal fight and concert he did. So tired of all the crap polluting minds out there. This *Change* guy isn't that. Has a message. A good message." He moved his arms in rhythm a few times back and forth in front of him. "Good beat. Easy to dance to."

This caused the three of us on the couch to look at each other with puzzled looks. Did Kenton crack a joke?

His voice continued to roar. "The organization he has started, I've done a lot of research about it, talked to a lot of people. Seems to be making a difference and growing. I like the idea and already we have different organizations and people from the community working with us. We have businesses offering job placement to the men getting out like I have never seen before. So! You let me know what you need and it's yours, even if I have to go break the arms of the Governor of this great state to get it. It's yours."

The contrast of the meaning of his words juxtaposed to how he said them had an astounding effect.

Adding to the contrast, Jeff's voice calmly replied, "Well you heard what I want, Warden, and I think you already have the idea. We will use the time these men are serving to build them up. I want to start a pilot program with this prison where we will educate these men, give them skills, teach them how to be a blessing to society. I want to draw the churches, community, and local colleges in the area into helping you give a chance for a decent life to these men. You, Luke, and Reverend Smith get together and figure out what the cost will be and it's yours. The *Invite The Change* program will cover any additional cost and provide the help you need. You don't need to go beat it out of the state. It will be taken care of."

The Warden leaned forward even more towards Jeff and glared at him. "Just like that? Magic? Dandy lions, butterflies, holding hands and singing happy songs?"

A short laugh came out before I could stop it.

Kenton stood straight up, snapped his head in my direction as he growled, "Glad you think I'm funny. Come back tomorrow. I'm here all week. Don't forget to tip the wait staff."

As much as I tried to hold it back another laugh came out. I held up my hand. "I'm so sorry. Please ignore me and go on."

His intense gaze stayed on me for a few uncomfortable seconds before turning to Jeff and blasting out his next statement. "Look! We've had plenty of 'the next greatest programs' here. Most fail spectacularly, causing more harm than good. Like I said, I did a lot of looking into this one and willing to give you a chance because I respect Reverend Smith and his trusts in you. But let me tell you." He walked around his desk, stood directly in front of Jeff, and leaned forward so he was face to face with Jeff. "If this program turns into 'just another program' I'll become an inmate here because I'll track you down and it won't be pretty."

I was waiting to hear how Jeff handled the threat, but before he could respond Luke stood up. "Warden, it'll be me you'll need to hold responsible and this will not be just another program."

Kenton stood and leaned against his desk with crossed arms as he studied Luke. Luke stood steady and stared back at the Warden as if there was a battle taking place in the air between their gazes.

After an intense minute of silence, I saw my first hint of a smile on Kenton's face as he stood and went back to his seat. Kenton held out his hands. "What do you need from me?"

Jeff spoke. "All I need from you, Warden, is a commitment to Reverend Smith and Luke for your support."

Kenton's voice pounded again with its harshness, "I'll teach classes myself if I have to. Reverend Smith and Luke have my unconditional support." His eyes went from each of us glaring. "Well, anything else? If not, get out, I have work to do."

I successfully held back the laugh this time. Every mannerism of his screamed anger but his actions and words were love. What an interesting man. Whoever tried to stand in the way of this program had my pity.

As the three of us rose from the cushy couch, Kent Kenton walked up to Reverend Smith, held his arms out and the old man went in and gave him a hug with the comfort of good, old friends. Kenton softly said, "Thanks for all you do. I will miss you when you are gone."

Reverend Smith replied, "Peace be with you, my old friend."

As Kenton released the hug, he held his fist out to Luke. Luke raised his own fist to meet the Warden's. Nothing else was said as we left.

Chapter 54

In the prison parking lot, as we were saying our good-byes to the four of them, I could tell they wanted to ask questions but none of them did. I am sure, in their minds, the questions would sound crazy, so no one chanced the subject as we said heartfelt goodbyes.

I didn't have the same reservations as the rest of them. As I turned out of the prison parking lot onto the road I said, "I'm sort of glad it isn't just me you're a jerk to."

Jeff smiled. "Glad I can make you happy."

"Two weeks ago? This was arranged two weeks ago?"

"Yeah."

"Yeah? That's it? Do you mind explaining why you sprung all of this on us?"

He slouched in his seat, leaned his head back, and closed his eyes. "Let me ask you this. Let's say I had called Luke two weeks ago and told him. What would have happened?"

As I worked my way back to the highway, I tried to work through the idea. "I don't know. Guess Luke and the Reverend would have been pretty excited. I mean, you got one of the biggest musical artists right now to come there. It is kind of a big deal."

"Yep. Keep going."

I wished I could have closed my eyes to picture this but that isn't conducive to driving. I tried to imagine Luke hearing this and then imagined us walking into the church today. Jeff had gotten *The Change* to come to the prison. It would be like me having the Rolling Stones playing at an event for me. "Today would have been about you and you getting Marcus to come."

He kept his eyes closed and head against the headrest. "Did you see how his parents and the Reverend viewed me? It was already too much about me." He sat up and looked at me. "This is about you, about Beth, about Luke, about Reverend Smith, Deon, Dylan, Grace, Keith, Aaron." He pointed out the window at the car I was passing. "It is about them. I cannot become the focal point of what is to come. What is to come is about each individual and their vertical growth. I can't become a Santa Claus passing out gifts. If it becomes that, people will wait up all night for me to come with the gift. The gift is yours already. My purpose is to point to the direction of the gift, not pass the gifts out."

I smiled. "Sounds like a problem another guy had. The people came to watch the miracles."

He nodded. "I'm not going to make that same mistake. Luke was cool today. He seems to get it. I'm sure you noticed him directing away from me being the focus today."

"Yeah, I did notice. It is amazing. When we met Luke on the side of the road that day I could have never envisioned him becoming what I saw today. He did seem to get it."

Jeff nodded his head. "Yeah, it's like everyone is a surprise package. Sometimes they are wrapped in a way that makes you think nothing's inside but then you open them up." He held his hand towards me. "Figuratively."

I gave a short laugh. "If you open them up literally they're just gooey and slimy, and it is most likely a felony."

"Right. But, if you can figure out how to open the package up, there's almost always something special inside."

As I checked my side mirror to change lanes I said, "Well, there is something special inside Luke." I looked over at Jeff and simply appreciated him as he looked out the front window. "Jeff?" He turned towards me. "Thanks for letting me see what was in that package."

He gave me a playful punch in the shoulder. "The awesome thing is, friend, it's Christmas year-round. We have a world full of packages to open. We just need to learn to see the beauty inside."

"That's the trick."

Jeff smiled but didn't reply.

I patted Jeff's shoulder. "You know, that's the first time I'd heard you preach if that's what you call it. That's the first time I've seen you front and center."

"The greatest leaders are the ones who aren't needed."

I let that gestate in my mind for a few miles. "Guess that kind of sums up HRI and your dad, too."

He gave me an approving look. "Exactly."

I let a few more miles mature my thoughts. "So, how does that fit with your work on Earth?" Considering I still hadn't figured out what Jeff was, that sounded strange coming from me. Yet, logically, he couldn't be anything else except a crazy man or a liar, yet those were far less believable so I was stuck with the paradox of believing logically until I believed spiritually.

Jeff took no notice of my internal conflict. "The same, I'm putting the people in place to make the changes that need to be made. I'll only be 'front and center' when it needs to happen and I'll go to the background as soon as I can. Like I said, this change is not about me, and if it were possible, I'd live an anonymous life with my family."

"Is it still pointless to ask why I'm one of those people you're putting in place? Because I'm still not seeing it."

Jeff answered with his unceasing smile, "Yep, still pointless. You're exactly the right person for what I need and you'll do what you need ..."

I interrupted, "... and I won't even know I'm doing it. Is it okay to tell you how much you piss me off?" I asked with my own smile.

"Absolutely okay, friend."

* * *

We drove until late, making it to Denver before stopping at a hotel for the night. I had a restless sleep wondering how I was going to do something great and not even know I was doing it. It just didn't make sense to me.

At about three in the morning, I grabbed the complimentary notepad, adjusted the pillows behind my back to rest against the headboard, and started writing down things that had happened since I met Jeff. After about an hour I had half of the pad filled with random events we'd experienced, ideas from the talks we've had, and anything else that came to mind. I set the pen down and read the pages over and over, trying to see how I fit in. It was a pointless effort because none of the events needed me. I was nothing more than a passenger. Sure, I learned a lot and grew a lot from the events and what I saw, but I couldn't see how that worked me into any master plan.

I slowly brought my feet to the side of the bed and stood up. Once that was done I wondered what to do next. I glanced at the TV but had no interest in watching anything. I looked around the hotel room at the limited options and decided some space and fresh air were better than pacing around in this small space. I slipped on my shorts and a shirt and stepped outside and leaned against the metal railing. It was a little too chilly for shorts and a T-shirt but that helped change my train of thought. The roar of a semi made me look out towards the highway. As my eyes followed it in its westward journey I looked down the highway more to see if I could see the Rockies yet, but it was still too dark.

Slowly I started walking and thinking about what Jeff wanted from me. Thankfully he said he didn't like the idea of standing on a street corner preaching his message. Yet, I didn't see myself becoming a preacher or an evangelist going door to door.

Imagining myself preaching Jeff's message in front of people made me realize something interesting; I wasn't sure what Jeff's message was. Sure, there was the conversation we had on salvation on the way out here and his unique extra-dimensional concept of Heaven and Hell, but those weren't what he was trying to get me to know. Those were more to release me from what was holding me back. He had a bigger message. I got to the railing at the end of the walkway and slowly started my way back. When I tried to think of the biggest takeaway from this whole strange experience, what kept coming to mind was Marcus' sermon on the Jonah Complex. I have been thinking about, or more precisely, still trying not to think about, how I never followed my destiny. That seemed to be where my mind was mostly.

Destiny, Jeff says I'm to do something great for him and tonight, with my little notepad half full, was the first time I really put any effort into figuring out what that is. I walked the length of the building again as I re-read the pages in the dim overhead lights. I gained no new insight. I did add 'connections', 'acceptance', 'destiny' before going back into my room and trying to go back to sleep.

* * *

It seemed like no sooner had I gotten back to sleep before there was a knock on the door and the evil morning sun was trying to come through the curtains. "Come in!" I yelled.

Jeff opened the locked door and walked in. He sat down on the chair by the table while I sat up and tried to wake up.

"Let me shower and I'll be ready to go." I grabbed my duffle bag and staggered to the bathroom.

"No problem, whenever you're ready. It's going to be a good day today. We can go see George at the bookstore. I always like seeing him," Jeff said with a sense of satisfaction.

"Cool," I replied as I shut the door to the bathroom, got in the shower, and put my face up towards the stream of steaming water trying to force myself into wakefulness.

When I came out Jeff was sitting in the chair looking at something in his hands. I got ready to go as he did that.

He interjected as I packed, "Hope you don't mind, I was looking at your notes."

"What notes?" I looked in his direction and saw the pad in his hands. I'd forgotten about that. "Oh yeah, I couldn't sleep last night so since you wouldn't tell me what I'm supposed to do for you ..." I did air quotes, "...you know, 'My destiny,' I thought I'd see if I could figure it out."

"Any luck?" he asked with his knowing smile.

I sneered at him in a joking way. "You know the answer to that and if you don't," I gave him a faux look of superiority and haughtily added, "I'm not going to tell you."

He laughed. "I think I'm being a bad influence on you. You're starting to sound like me."

I picked up my stuff and headed towards the door. "That would be bad. One of you is too many. Come on, let's get breakfast."

* * *

We grabbed a quick breakfast and got on our way to see George. I found myself looking forward to that. I didn't get to enjoy the store the first time, but it looked like one of those truly unique places that seemed to just feel right for some unknown reason. The last time we were there, I'd been in a perpetual state of shock and had hoped George would help me understand Jeff, but in the end, George's stories had only added to my confusion.

I glanced over at Jeff sitting beside me looking like a normal person resting with his eyes closed and a book on his lap. In the time between leaving George's on the trip east, and now coming back, what more did I know about him? He took me through time and space when I freaked out about leaving HRI. That was slightly major. He was adopted and lost his much loved adopted parents before he was nineteen. Had a house full of adopted kids that ran like clockwork but with very individualistic people. It wasn't a military routine, tightly controlled. It was a bunch of individuals who felt they should be helping make the house someplace safe and special. HRI was the same, a bunch of individuals working to build something great. He had a very cool butler who seemed to know more than he was letting on. Jeff had built a six-stroke engine in his workshop before a team of genius HRI engineers could.

My list grew and grew but none of it seemed to answer much about Jeff. I guess what I wanted was for him to come down from the sky with a golden glow around him and say, 'I am Jeff Havens, sent by <insert sender here> to do <insert task here> and I have chosen you to <insert my role here>.' But instead, I got a prankster keeping me off balance my whole time with him.

So, between stops to George's, I'd learned about him, grown to love him with a more profound sense of love than I could have imagined before, but I didn't have the solid answers I would have liked to have.

A voice beside me said, "Golden glow descending from the clouds? Really? You don't think it's too theatrical?"

My head snapped towards him. "What? Really? Don't you think that's over-the-top rude?"

He opened his eyes and rolled his head towards me. "Friend, you were thinking pretty loud. It was hard not to."

I looked at him but didn't smile.

He poked my shoulder with his fingertips. "Come on, friend. Lighten up."

"I don't get any privacy?"

I shrugged. "I try, but they're just waves. It's like asking me not to hear people talking or see something. I can close my eyes or cover my ears but I can't shut that sense down, I can only ignore it."

That answer caught me off guard and changed my anger to curiosity. "Waves? But what happens in rooms with a lot of people? You have the sound, vision, and a room full of brain waves?"

He scooched up from his resting position and put a bookmark in his book. "At first it was unnerving but over time it just becomes part of the experience."

"But that has to be a lot of information for a brain to process."

His head moved up and down affirming my statement. "Yes, for a brain working in this dimension it would be impossible. Move up one dimension, space and time expand exponentially. It's manageable."

My mind exploded with new questions. "So, for me, can I ..."

"Hey, you get to see the Rockies this time. You passed out last time and I drove through them."

My mind shot back to the cruel lottery ticket prank at the gas station on the trip out east. Jeff had me so wired up and confused that my mind shut down. I use that lottery ticket as a bookmark now. Not sure exactly why, but it always carried a hidden meaning for me. I started to speak but then I wondered why Jeff brought up the situation right then. He had never mentioned it before. I sighed, "I'm not ready? Too much for me?"

Jeff looked me in the eye and I tried to return the gaze and still stay on the road. "You're more ready than most but it isn't your time or your destiny."

"I'm not ready to subtract big numbers from little numbers yet?"

He gave a warm laugh. "You're ready for much more than that. You're a great man with great wisdom but your contribution to *the change* is something different than mine. Just worry about doing your role."

I let out another sigh. "I know where this conversation goes. I ask what that is, and you obfuscate."

"Pretty much. So, let's enjoy the Rockies."

I smiled and turned my attention fully to driving. Thankfully it was a short distance from Denver before we left the high plains and got to the foothills of the Rockies. After a long, beautiful, twisty, windy, yet unchallenged drive, we got to St. George, Utah, and pulled up to the bookstore around dinnertime.

When I got out of the car, the heat surprised me. Over the top of the car, I remarked to Jeff, "It's hotter than I expected."

"Ninety-six on the thermometer back a little way."

I joined him on the sidewalk as we walked to the store. "It was cool this morning in Denver. Expected September to be cooler here."

"Yeah, it was nice this morning. Mid-nineties are about normal here this time of year." Jeff opened the bookstore door for a woman leaving and then held it for me.

As I walked in I looked at the oversized 'living room' area with over half the seats occupied. I was about to comment on what a cool area that was when I heard George call our names. I looked to the left towards the dining area and saw him walk his aging body from behind the counter. We took a left turn towards the counter with the antique soda fountain and met George part way. He gave Jeff an affectionate hug, then came to me and gave me an equally affectionate hug.

I guess by association with Jeff I was deserving also. Like his bookstore, George was someone who just seemed right for some unknown reason. He had such a sense of peace and contentment about him.

He looked at Jeff with a hopeful expression. "Can you stay longer this time? Last time you rushed out."

Jeff looked at me to answer the question.

With a smirk, I asked Jeff, "We don't have an appointment I don't know about that we're late for?"

"No, just have to get to Sally's wedding in Barstow in time."

With a grin, I looked at George. "Can we make it to Barstow by Saturday?"

He brought his hands together in front of him. "Oh, let's see. It's Thursday now and you have about three hundred miles." He looked up like he was doing some calculations. "If you can keep your average speed over fifteen miles per hour I think you'll do okay."

I nodded. "I think we can do that."

Before George even started talking he grabbed my arm and led me towards a table to the left of the soda fountain. "Oh, Good. Let me get you something to eat." He waved a young man over to take our orders.

George pointed out a couple of his favorites so the ordering didn't take long. As the waiter walked away I turned to George. "I really like your store. It's so different than most bookstores or even other stores in general."

George looked at me with interest. "Do you read much?"

I nodded. "I've been reading more lately. Hope I can keep that pattern going."

"That's good. Reading people are interesting people. But maybe I'm biased." He gave a wide grin.

Jeff interjected, "He's a writer, too."

George's eyes filled with excitement.

I gave Jeff an exasperated look. "A tech writer, Jeff."

"And a very good one. And didn't you write when you were younger? Your degree was to teach writing, wasn't it?"

George got more excited. "You taught writing? This is exceptional! What a wonderful thing to teach."

Now I was more exasperated but tried to hide it. "I taught literature for my student teaching but realized teaching wasn't my path."

George was not detoured by me minimizing my experience. "Taught literature? That's just as good. If you lived closer, I'd invite you to teach a class here at the store. We host several writing and literature classes."

I paused for a few seconds as I thought about that. "You know, it's too bad I don't live closer. I'd enjoy that. It would be fun to teach people who really want to learn."

"Oh, it's exceptional. It's a very popular thing here."

Jeff changed the direction. "Why don't you write anymore? I'll bet you'd be a good writer."

George was interested in the answer so I changed the snide reply I was going to give Jeff to a more sincere reply. "Guess life gets in the way. I don't have the desire to write like when I was younger."

George gave an understanding nod. "That's too bad. I'll bet Jeff's right."

We were interrupted as the young man brought us our drinks. Before he left George asked him to bring us some Baklava.

Approvingly I said, "I'm always in the mood for Baklava."

George grinned. "Then you'll like this. A local bakery makes it. We get a lot of our baked goods there. The bread from the Panini you ordered is from there. The meat is from a meat processing plant nearby I'm especially fond of. We try to support the local places. Some of our dishes come from the restaurant across the street."

I looked at him questioning. "You have a strange idea of competition."

He shook his head. "No, never competition. Always collaboration. There's plenty to go around. Instead of trying to get a bigger piece of the pie, we all work together to make the pie bigger."

I took a drink as I thought about that.

Chapter 55

Our food came and we chatted as we ate. Jeff took the last bite of his sandwich, wiped his mouth, and pushed back his chair. "Well, I've some shopping to do. Need to do my part to keep the economy going and support mom and pop shops. Right, Pop?" Jeff moved away laughing.

As George and I watched him leave George shook his head. "Don't let him fool you."

I turned and looked at him confused and a bit hopeful. Was someone finally going to out Jeff for not being everything he appeared to be?

George continued, "This store was bought by an investment firm about ten years ago. I was fighting a losing battle to keep it open and I put it up for sale. Right away, in came some guys in suits, looking around and asking questions."

I raised my eyebrows.

"They took pictures, measured things. You know, kicking tires type of things. Then they did something strange. They asked me, in my ideal store, what would I want?" He smiled. "That was a silly thing to do. I always had dreams for this place I couldn't do because feeding my family was kind of important to me. I couldn't invest the money. And to be honest, once the kids were grown, the dream sort of died. Or, I thought it had. Being asked the question brought back the dream into my mind."

I watched as his dream lit up his eyes. I didn't want to interrupt so I just nodded.

"I told them I wanted an antique soda fountain, I wanted to expand into the building next door, I wanted an eating area and reading area. I wanted to replace all my bookshelves with antique shelves. I went on and on as they took notes." He shook his head. "Then they left. I spent the whole night cursing myself for talking too much. My grandkids were spending some time with us so my wife took them to the movies just to get away from me."

First, I tried to imagine this man not being someone people wanted to spend time with. Then I glanced around the store and added, "Guess I know how the story ends. You got to build the store you dreamed of."

He reached over and placed his hand on my forearm. "Let me tell you, it was hard to come in the next day. I just knew I'd lost my chance out of a money pit. But soon after I unlocked the doors, the suited group walked in. They placed an offer on the counter. They loved my vision and wanted to put me on salary to make it happen. Never heard, 'no' for anything I've asked for and never had to look at finances again."

With a smile, he turned and looked at Jeff who was scanning over books a few aisles away. "Don't let him fool you. This is his bookstore and he gave it to me as a gift."

I drank the last bit of my drink as I looked at Jeff. "Ten years ago, huh?" Jeff would have been back from his roaming.

"Yes, haven't worried a lick about anything but making a great book store for ten wonderful years." George gently poked me in the shoulder. "And, he still insists on buying the books. Gives me a dumb look if I mention the investment company."

Well, I thought, so much for anybody painting a picture of Jeff other than that of the one I've already witnessed.

I looked over at Jeff and his growing stack of books, just the opposite of the point he was making at the shopping mall. I glanced at the people talking at the nearby tables, then towards some people playing chess at a table near the reading area, and looking up to the shelves themselves were people browsing books together. The words, connection, community, and acceptance came to mind. When I thought about the mall, those words didn't fit. To me, the strip mall felt artificial and contrived, but the store of George's dream felt like community, a place of connections and acceptance. I made a mental note to add community to my list of words.

George excused himself to go help at the checkout counter so I decided to walk around some. Making my way down the well-worn hardwood floors, I ran my fingers across the binding of some books aligned neatly on one of the many ancient-looking oak bookshelves and then pushed the rolling ladder to the end of the aisle. A man sitting on one of the many antique sofas looked up as I walked by and greeted me with a nod.

After about twenty minutes, I had finished my appreciation phase of the store and was now ready to do some serious shopping. One of the very few advantages of being away from my family and living in a hotel room is I had time to read. In the past two months, I'd read more books than I had in the past five years. My appetite for reading had increased.

Jeff was so big on books. He handed them out like candy. So, it wasn't a surprise to notice titles he had handed out. I reached out and pulled a used copy of *Flatland: A Romance of Many Dimensions* off the shelf. There must have been thirty copies and many different editions. The copy I held was the same edition Jeff bought for me two months ago from this very spot. As I thumbed through the discolored pages it brought me back to my first days with Jeff. In some ways, I'd quit trying to figure out what Jeff was. I just let Jeff be Jeff and tried to learn what I could from him. I think trying to understand what Jeff is was an impossible task. If he is a fourth-dimensional being, I don't think that would change what he is here to teach me or what task he wants me to do for him. So, Jeff is Jeff, a magnificent being and the biggest pain in the butt I've ever met. As I closed the book and put it in with the other copies I silently said thanks to the forces which put him into my life.

Jeff's voice snapped me back from inside my mind. "Stanley? Did I lose you in there somewhere?"

I jumped and looked at him for a second. "Just thinking that I should've run that light two months ago in Bakersfield."

"I never told you this, but the next car coming to that light was a beautiful brunette, single and about my age. This whole fate thing isn't always what it's cracked up to be. I got stuck with you because you stopped."

I scoffed, "You saying you got the short end of this deal?"

"Absolutely, friend."

I raised my hand and bopped him gently on the head. "Good. You deserve it." I turned and started walking slowly down the aisle and Jeff strolled with me. On the shelf to my left, there were several copies of Hermann Hesse's *Siddhartha*. I took one and looked at it. "I think I saw this in your library."

"I wouldn't be surprised. I can't even imagine how many copies of that I've given away."

"You know, that's something I've always wondered. You give away a lot of books but they always seem random."

"I give people books to read because, at the time I do, they're looking very hard for answers and ready to hear the answers. It doesn't matter what book. When your mind is ready to hear an answer, you'll find it in almost anything you read. I do pick some books on purpose because they give the message stronger. *Siddhartha* is an example of that. But most of the time, any random book will have the answer you're ready to hear. The main thing is to have questions and want answers."

"I've never had a shortage, but answers are hard to come by." With a smile, I took the copy I was holding and started walking down some more aisles with Jeff.

Once I felt I was supporting George enough, Jeff and I headed to the checkout area. We passed a table with some notebooks, so I grabbed one of those and some pens. I'd started some notes on the hotel's notepad but that wasn't going to be enough to start looking at the events and figuring out what Jeff had planned for me.

George met us at the counter.

Jeff put his stuff there and indicated for me to do the same. "I guess we're set, George. Glad we had more time to spend with you this time."

George replied, "Oh, me too and I'm glad you don't look as bad as you did last time. You were a mess. Make sure you stop in again sometime, Stanley."

He rang us up. I pulled out my wallet but Jeff put two hundred dollar bills on the counter and motioned for me to put my wallet back. George looked at him and sighed.

Jeff said, "Just let that go as far as it can with the next customers."

George just shook his head, made the change, and placed it to the side of the register. Then he came around the counter and walked with us to the door where we said our final goodbyes.

After unlocking the car, we both put our bags behind the seat. Once in the car, Jeff said, "We're doing good time-wise. You just want to relax here the rest of the day and we can take off in the morning? I think the break from driving would be nice."

I nodded in agreement, "Yeah, that would be good."

Chapter 56

I slept hard that night but must have stayed up until one o'clock reading *Siddhartha*. It was nine o'clock before I even looked at the clock. The book fell on the floor as I pulled myself out of bed, but I left it and walked to the window. Moving the curtain a crack, I squinted my eyes from the light. There was Jeff sitting with his feet in the pool while reading. Just to the left of the pool was the Jetta, still wet and shiny from a fresh wash. I knew it had a full tank of diesel, also.

Turning from the window I bumped into the table and the Jetta keys fell to the floor. This caused me to smile. Driving the Jetta without keys is a cool trick. I left those on the floor with the book and lazily stumbled to the shower.

It was nine-thirty before I started down the motel steps. Jeff watched me walk down the stairs with my duffle bag. When I got close enough to hear he said, "Friday is wasting away, friend. By my calculations, we have two hundred and seventy-six miles to cover."

Doing my own quick calculations, I replied. "So, we'll be there in time for dinner. Relax."

The restaurant we had breakfast at was exceptionally fast and good. Just after ten o'clock, back at the Jetta, I threw Jeff the keys. "I know you don't need these but I'm sure you can understand the symbolism."

"Reading time. I get it," he answered. We hopped in the Jetta and we were on our way again.

But the reading was soon interrupted. We weren't more than ten minutes on the road before Jeff pointed up ahead. "The Virgin River Gorge."

I looked up from *Siddhartha* and saw the terrain start to turn into high plateaus. I put my lottery ticket bookmark in, closed the book, and put it in my lap. "Yeah, I enjoyed this on the trip out. A very interesting drive."

"A million dollars a mile to build this in the late seventies. One of the most expensive roads ever built," said Jeff.

"You should be a tour guide."

"Yep, I missed my calling. The current gig is pretty taxing."

I smiled and watched the scene change and imagined the blasting that was needed to remove the rocks for the road. It exposed millions of years of strata and showed the movement of the strata over that time. In some ways, the work done had added to nature's beauty by making it visible to all.

As we started coming out of the gorge I looked at Jeff. "I think your current gig is a tour guide, isn't it? I mean, you've spent that last couple of months pointing things out to me."

He nodded his head thoughtfully. "I like the analogy. Maybe I didn't miss my calling."

* * *

I alternated between reading the books I bought from George's store and revising my list of events with Jeff in the notebook I also bought there. But after a while I found myself watching the desert landscape as we passed. I looked at Jeff. "Can you pull over somewhere?"

He pointed up ahead. "There's a road up here. Is that okay?"

"Sure."

Jeff turned down the road and stopped.

He picked a good spot. I walked out into the sand for a ways and climbed one of the hills. My companion followed me without any questions. I turned and looked deeper into the desert. Small plants and shrubs were all around with a few of them flowering. I walked up to a flowering plant and watched a butterfly land on the flower.

"Not many flowers," I said without looking up.

"September's not a great month for that. March and April are much better."

I didn't respond but instead closed my eyes and focused on the gentle wind and the sun hitting me. It was hot but not as piercing as it was a couple of months ago. Every few seconds I could hear a car passing but other than that there was a calm quiet ruling the desert.

Finally, a voice broke the silence. "You picked an interesting place to stop. You know this isn't too far from where you ran off the road after we left Vegas?"

Turning, I gave him a look. "Really?"

"Yep. So, what's up? Why did we stop?"

I smiled at this. I appreciated Jeff playing human. He knows why I stopped but I voiced it as much for me as him. "Can't really say. It just seems like I've driven through the deserts without ever really noticing anything. But as I was looking out the windows I saw a beauty I'd never seen before." This reminded me of something Jeff had said when we first met. He was talking about taking a bicycle trip because you got to see the country instead of zooming through it. I started walking further away from the road. The heat wasn't too bad. Maybe in the low nineties.

I turned to Jeff. "I need to stop more often. I need to stop and just look and notice."

Jeff was looking deep out into the distance. "We aren't programmed to do that. We rush from point A to point B and the trip is just an obstacle."

Kneeling, I took a handful of sand. It was coarse and I let it fall through my fingers. "Programmed and obstacles." I turned to him. "Will that ever change?"

He shrugged. "Only if people want it to."

A melancholy stream seemed to flow through me. I reached over and brushed a plant. I wasn't sure what it was called. But my mind drifted to car payments and jobs and mortgages and kids school and electric bills and meetings and food bills and trying to find time to fit life between the cracks of making a living. I stood and looked at him. "I suck at this."

Again, he shrugged. "Most do. Reprogramming is hard. Don't beat yourself up about it. If it makes you feel any better, the man I left Bakersfield with didn't stop."

This brought me a smile. "No. He didn't, did he? Maybe there's hope."

He put his arm around me. "More than you know, friend. More than you know."

Without either of us leading or following we made our way back to the car and, for a short time, I lived in the moment.

* * *

Jeff drove through Vegas and I tried to appreciate it for what it was, but in truth, the mountains, the gorge, the desert were interesting but Vegas, nothing about it carried any meaning for me.

As we got to the west side of Las Vegas, we passed the hotel where we spent the first night. Jeff hit the blinker and said, "Lunchtime."

This reminded me I was getting hungry until I saw where he was going. With a look of sheer panic, I begged, "No, Jeff! No, don't do this to me."

"Relax," he said with his calm smile. "It'll be fine." He pulled in front of the building where the biker bar had been but this time there were only a few bikes in a clearly marked motorcycle parking area. The building, instead of black, had a new bright white paint job and a new sign, "Zack's Family Fun and Perfect Pizza." The part of the sign that said: "Zack's" was still the same but the "Family Fun and Perfect Pizza" was tacked to the end in an ill-fitting way. We pulled up and got out of the car.

I looked over at Jeff with a questioning look, "So, what's up here?"

"Let's go find out and have some 'Perfect Pizza'," answered Jeff.

We walked in and, although I recognized the layout, the tables, the dartboards, the pool tables, this time the place was bright and cheerful in stark contrast to the last time we were here. There were a large number of people in the place, and as the sign advertised, they seemed to be mostly families. The pool tables and dartboards were almost all taken with what looked like families. The sign said, "Seat yourself" so Jeff and I found a table, sat down, picked up the menu on the table, and started looking it over. They had sandwiches, burgers, and other choices besides pizza.

Jeff said, "I don't know about you, but any place that says they have 'perfect pizza', it seems like we should have pizza."

"I'm never one to turn down pizza but it was pretty bad last time," I said as the waiter came to the table.

He did not stand there; he pulled up a chair and sat down. He had a long gray ponytail and a long gray but a neatly groomed beard. He was wearing a T-shirt with the restaurant's logo and name on it with the sleeves cut off allowing us to see the ancient tattoos on his arms. "Well, look what the cat dragged in," he said. I looked at him and it took a little while to place him, he was the bartender and owner from when we were here last time.

Seeing Zack started bringing back the fear and memories from our first time here. I felt my heart rate go up and an uneasiness form in my stomach.

Calmly Jeff inquired, "So, we aren't getting out of here unnoticed?"

"Oh no! I've been waiting for the day when you two might walk through that door again. I knew when you left last time that wouldn't be the last I saw of you guys." He smiled and shook his head. "That was the craziest crap I'd ever seen. And the timing? Man, the timing."

He paused and Jeff did not say anything so I asked, "How's that?"

"I'd been running this dive for thirty-seven years. When I was young and rebellious, it seemed like what I wanted to do. Age changes a man. The things I was seeing here started bothering me." Zack looked at the ground and thought. "I don't know. It was bad stuff." He looked back up at Jeff and then me. There were a lot of thoughts going on but he let them stay in his head. He leaned back in the chair and let his shoulders drop. "'Bout a year ago, I start slipping into churches after they started and leaving before they ended. You know, listening for something. Something that would give me something different. Musta gone to ten different churches hoping to hear that something." He let out a sigh. "In some ways, they felt as empty as my bar. I felt like they are trying to say something important but just not saying it. Anyways, I knew I couldn't keep going the way I was going and had to figure it out." He leaned forward, put his elbows on the table, and grinned. "Then you two walked in. The next day I didn't have a choice."

He had stopped again to reflect but I was wondering what did happen after we left. I had wondered about Bear but hadn't thought about the broader picture. "What happened when we left?" I asked.

"Depends on how you want to look at it. Not much or a lot. Not much, in that the bar just about died because Bear, the man who pounded you that night, was a driving force in most that was wrong in this area. You can't even begin to imagine the night and day change he went through. In my thirty-seven years of running this dive, he scared me more than anyone else that had ever been in here. The next day he wasn't here and his gang wasn't here. I didn't know he was such a big player in the drug trade around here. A big part of the drugs in the area dried up overnight." Zack held up his hands beside him and shrugged. "And because of that my business dried up. So, I was going out of business fast. The funny thing was, I didn't mind. I sat here in an empty bar for a week thinking about it."

I leaned back in my chair and scanned the place. A dad was leaning over a pool table with his daughter, teaching her how to break. That same table, just a couple of months ago, was in a different world. A young mother was holding a baby while pushing buttons on the old jukebox looking for songs to play. The place was painted bright and friendly with light coming through the windows adding to the florescent lighting coming from the ceiling. This was the type of place I could see bringing my family to.

I turned to Zack. "I guess you figured it out."

"Yeah, put a sign in the window 'Closed for remodeling', bought a bunch of cheap paint, and went to work on the outside. Within a couple of hours, Bear and his gang descended on my bar with paintbrushes and hammers and this is what we got."

We looked around. The fresh paint made a difference but there was still work to do. I wasn't going to burst Zack's bubble though because he was moving in the right direction and things like this take time and money.

Zack then looked at Jeff very intensely for an uncomfortable minute. "I witnessed a miracle that day. I have no idea who you are but what you did was from God. Nothing else could have allowed you to stand up to Bear like you did. You should've died after the first punch. And then to have his old man come here and to see Bear cry, to see him become a new man, I witnessed a miracle. Do you remember what you said to me?" he directed the question at Jeff.

Jeff shrugged but didn't indicate either way.

"I know exactly what you said because when you witness a miracle like I did, you listen to the words of the person performing the miracle. You said, 'Had a great time here tonight. Except for the pizza. You really need to work on that.' I have no idea why God wants me making pizza but, if God is going to tell me to make pizza, I'm going to make the best pizza ever. I found a good deal on a used pizza oven and now I make a perfect pizza."

I smiled inside my head because I didn't want to look like I was laughing at Zack. He was dead serious. And really, I wasn't laughing at him at all, but instead had a great amount of respect for him. He did witness a miracle that day, drew a very logical conclusion, and acted on it. He was not suffering from the Jonah Complex like me but instead embracing his destiny.

He continued, "I figured since I was doing it I would really do it. I have a conference/party room back there and now instead of serving alcohol to alcoholics, I serve pizza to recovering alcoholics at their weekly AA meetings. The community support has been overwhelming. We are now hosting church youth groups every Wednesday night and Bear and his group try to make it here for that as often as they can. You should see those teens playing pool with those bikers. It's one of the strangest, most bizarre, yet heartwarming, sights you've ever seen. I can't say I'm making as much money but it's enough and I feel great."

"And you make a perfect pizza, right?" Jeff asked.

"Wait until you try it. I dug and dug to find out how to make great pizza. It became an obsession. I'm planning on building a brick oven when I get some extra cash. But, even with the second-hand pizza oven, you'll never find a better pizza. Whenever I can, I use organic, locally grown tomatoes and other vegetables but we live in a freakin' dessert so I do the best I can. The herbs come right out of my garden. I modified what I have been growing if you know what I mean. We have a choice of four different kinds of mushrooms and none of the magic kind you used to find in this place. The sausage and other meats come from a free-range farm. I'm even working with a dairy to start making cheese for me. This pizza's gonna blow your mind it is so good, and it's on the house for you guys." With that, he got up and went off to make our pizza without even asking what kind we wanted.

I looked at Jeff. "God told him to make pizza?"

Jeff looked at me almost insulted. "It's pizza. Of course, God would want that."

I wanted to laugh but I wasn't sure if he was joking. I pointed to the pool tables. "Pool?"

"Sure. I'll rack. You put some music on. See if they have *Spirit in the Sky*. Seems fitting for this occasion."

As I expected, the song was there and the heavily distorted guitar started soon after I entered the number. I grabbed a cue and checked to see if it was straight.

Jeff tossed me the cue ball. "You break."

I placed the cue ball a little off-center and lined up to break. It was a decent break and I sunk the four ball. That left me lined up for the six and I made it easy. But after that, I had nothing. I tried a complicated combination shot but it didn't even come close. In reality, my mind was somewhere else. I watched Jeff examine the table as I thought back to the events which took place in this building our first time here.

Jeff got my attention with, "ten in the corner pocket."

I looked at the shot, which was overly difficult, and I wondered why he didn't shoot the twelve. It was a straight shot. I watched him put the ten in which left him a great shot at the fifteen and then a great shot at the eleven, then the twelve, and that pattern continued until the eight ball. The game was over. Jeff ran the table.

I sneered at him and went to put my cue up.

"One more game," Jeff said.

Somewhat irritated, I asked, "What's the point? You're obviously a shark. I can't win."

Calmly Jeff motioned me back as he put some change into the table. "This is Jeff you're talking to, Stanley. There's always a point."

"Humiliation is usually your point with me."

He cocked his head to the side. "It may be this time too, but let me give you some pointers on your game."

Slowly I walked back as he racked the balls. He then gave a decent break but didn't sink anything. The table was open and I had a choice of balls. The six was the easiest so I lined up.

Jeff's voice stopped me. "Why that shot?"

With a confused look, I answered, "Because, I can make it."

He brought his shoulders up. "Then what?"

Still confused I answered. "I look for the next shot and take it."

Jeff leaned against the empty table next to us. "A while back, we had a talk on the roof patio at HRI, you talked about the Iroquois and the concept of planning actions today based on how it affects seven generations down the road. Do you remember?"

"Nope. I know the concept but don't remember talking about it." Then, with a look of understanding, I jokingly said, "But, I can see where this is going. I should look at this pool game to see how it affects my decedents. Their lives could depend on me winning or not."

Ignoring my joke Jeff pointed at the table. "No, just a good metaphor. Seven balls, seven generations." He walked to the other side of the table. "So, the six is easy but there's nowhere to go from there. Pool is a game of action and reaction. If you plan your action with the proper reaction you have a better chance of winning. Look at the three. It's a relatively easy shot and if you hit it soft enough you're set up for the five, which sets you up for the four, which sets you up for the … well, you get the idea."

I looked around reevaluating the table. Then I looked up and around the bar and reevaluated. Jeff didn't care about a pool game. He was making a point. I saw Zack sitting at a table talking to some customers. He was down on one knee talking to a boy about six years old as his parents listened. It was like a light went off in my head. "Zack was shooting at the six ball a couple of months ago. There was nowhere for him to go after that shot." I scanned the place again. "But you gave him a better shot that night. One where the reaction has possibilities."

Jeff nodded. "Yep."

I leaned down, lined up on the three, pushed my pool cue through the cue ball gently so it would stay near the point of contact with the three. I did it perfectly and had a shot at the five. But to be set up for the four I needed to hit just off-center with a little spin. I lined up the tip of my pool cue and took the shot. The cue ball went perfectly to the place I wanted and I had a beautiful shot at the four. There was only one problem. The five hit the bumper and didn't go in.

From off to my side I hear, "Lesson number two. If you spend too much time focusing on the reaction and that causes you to mess up the action, you lose."

I watched Jeff with a new interest as he masterfully handled the actions and reactions of the game and ran the table.

"One more time," I said.

That turned into three more times and would have kept going if the pizza hadn't come. I never got a second chance to shoot in any of the games but my action-reaction planning improved exponentially.

With the pizza beckoning us to the table, Jeff and I sat down and dug in. I love pizza and have eaten it all over America, but this was hands down the best pizza ever. I'm not sure how he did it but Zack did make the perfect pizza. Jokingly to myself, I thought, "When God picks someone to make a pizza, God sure knows who to pick."

We were getting up to go, Jeff reached in his pocket and pulled out some money when Zack came up behind us, placing a strong hand on each of our shoulders, and said, "If you even leave a tip I'll throw you through that door." Being a wise man Jeff put the money back in his pocket and Zack walked with us to the door with his hands still on our shoulders and said, "If I ever hear you've passed within a hundred miles of here, and didn't stop in to see me, and get your free pizza, I'll send Bear and his hooligans after ya and I'm not responsible for what happens."

"We wouldn't dream of it," I said.

As Jeff and I walked to the car I asked, "What about Bear? Do we get to see how he came out of this?"

"You heard Zack, didn't you? Bear's doing fine."

As I opened my door I started to push the point but after the last couple of months, I knew him well enough to know this was Jeff-speak for 'wait and see'. I turned back to look at Zack's Family Fun and Perfect Pizza. I stood with one arm on top of the car and the other on top of the doorframe and tried to remember what it was like when Jeff and I had first stopped here. In just two months it was totally transformed.

I looked over at Jeff who was looking in the same direction. I said, "That was a good pizza. Thanks for taking me here."

He directed his gaze towards me. "There is a lot of good in this world, Stanley."

I smiled gratefully in response as we slid into our seats.

As we drove I thought about the pool game strategy, the Iroquois seventh-generation philosophy, and how Zack's previous establishment was about the easy —here and now— with little thought about the long-term future. But it didn't take long for me to realize I was no better than Zack. I have a long history of taking the easy path at the cost of my future, much less seven generations. Who could plan actions and reactions and how they would affect seven generations?

* * *

Just outside Primm, Nevada we passed the sign welcoming us to California. The emotional reaction I had to the sign shocked me. I was almost home. After two and a half very strange months I was going to be home with my family. Yet I wouldn't see them for another day or two. It was Friday now, Sally's wedding was sometime Saturday and I wasn't going to try to predict when we would leave Barstow.

We passed a sign saying Barstow was 111 miles away. Barstow was only a couple of hours from Bakersfield. A big part of me wanted to just drive to Bakersfield today and come back to Barstow tomorrow for the wedding. Yet, deep down, I knew reaching Bakersfield was a symbolic end to my time with Jeff, and seeing Sally had to happen before that end. I have a lifetime ahead of me with my family but I wasn't sure what was going to happen with Jeff when I got home. Would he and I stay in contact?

I looked over at him. He had leaned back the seat and had his eyes closed. This was one of the few times he wasn't reading while I drove. Turning my attention back to the road, as I stared through the windshield, a heaviness settled in my mind. This was ending. What will happen when we reach Bakersfield? I started to move my mouth to ask that question but then stopped. I was telling myself there was no chance Jeff would answer that question, but in reality, it wasn't a question I wanted answered. It was all part of the experience. With that thought, I took a deep breath, relaxed my shoulders, and continued my way down Interstate 15.

Chapter 57

We pulled into Barstow on Friday. Sally's wedding was tomorrow, so we had plenty of time. We checked into a hotel and Jeff suggested we relax a bit before getting some dinner. That sounded like a good idea to me so I grabbed some stuff from the car and, once in the hotel room, I made use of the overly firm mattress to ease the tension of hundreds of miles of riding.

I called Beth to let her know we made it this far and was impressed with how understanding she was.

"Any idea when you'll be home? You heading here tomorrow, after the wedding?" she asked.

I gave a soft laugh. "I hate to even predict. If I tell you something it'll change for sure. I can push for tomorrow."

Beth replied with her own soft laugh. "No, don't push it. You have a story to tell your grandchildren. I don't think the ending should be, 'and then I cut it all short because I wanted to rush home'."

A smile came to my face with that thought. I did have a story to tell. "Okay, let's plan for tomorrow, and if it changes I'll let you know."

We talked for a bit more before ending the call. I couldn't help but feel anxiety take control of me as I thought about my future with Beth. Ever since Jeff and I had the conversation where he wouldn't answer the question about her and me, there has been an uneasiness I had been pushing down and ignoring. How could things not work with her? She was handling every detour of our plans with grace. I was going to lay down and try to push this fear to the back of my mind again but then saw my notebook and picked it up. This was a far better way to distract my brain. The few notes I was going to make ended up being the whole experience at Zack's. I smiled as I wondered how my actions of writing about that experience would affect seven generations down the road.

My thoughts were interrupted by a knock on my door. I yelled, "Come in." As I watched Jeff open the locked door it occurred to me this would most likely be the last time I saw him do that.

"I want to make a stop before we get some dinner. You good with that, friend?"

I closed the notebook on my pen to mark where I left off and set it on the nightstand. "Sure. That's fine." I swung my legs off the bed. "Dinner? We going to see Sally?"

"Yeah, we can do that if you want but do you think she'd be working the day before her wedding?"

I stood and started towards the door. "Guess we'll find out."

When we were closer to the car I pulled out my keys and Jeff held out his hand. That was fine with me. It was better than having him guide me to where he wanted to go.

He drove through some residential areas and because I wasn't driving I was able to just look around. This area, being in the Mohave desert, offered a challenge to homeowners. There was very little grass on most lawns and the few with green lawns looked out of place with the dirt lawns of their neighbors.

"It's like there's a war going on," I said quietly as we drove.

"What?" Jeff asked.

I turned and looked at him. "Oh, sorry. I was just muttering to myself."

"About?"

I pointed out the window. "Look. Green grass in the desert. It's man versus nature. And right next door to that, dirt. Nature won."

Jeff didn't respond but we both looked out the window as we drove.

He pulled up in front of a house and shut off the car. I stepped out of the car onto some light-colored crushed stone and then stepped onto one of the darker natural stone pavers leading to the front door. I stopped and looked at the interesting tree, about twenty feet tall, to the right of the path. "Joshua tree."

"Looks good in the yard. Maybe a peace treaty was signed here." He pointed. "Cottonwood. Another native." Then he pointed to another part of the yard where a darker crushed stone created a distinct contrast to the lighter stone next to it. "Chaparral yucca, desert holly, California juniper. All native plants. She's done a nice job integrating them into the yard."

The —she— in his sentence jumped out at me. I realized I never even questioned Jeff as to who we were coming to see. But I let that pass and just repeated Jeff's words. "Peace treaty."

Jeff looked around the yard. "Yeah." Then he turned and made his way up the stone walkway to the front door and rang the bell.

Now the —she— question took on more brain activity. My first thought was Sally but Jeff would have told me if we were coming to see her. This was his way of playing games with my mind. It was going to be a surprise I didn't see coming. I tried to think of all the women we had met and which of them might be in Barstow.

A lady in her late 50's came to the door. She had her hair pulled back and some gardening gloves on her hands. She didn't look familiar so now my mind was working on Jeff's twist to this.

In a very pleasant and welcoming voice, the woman said, "May I help you?"

"Is Harris around?" Jeff asked.

I wanted to let out a laugh but held it back. Jeff got me. Harris, the high school boy on the cliff at Zion National Park, had never even entered my mind. Now that we were here it seemed obvious we should come to see him.

This also made me think about my notes. I had forgotten about Harris in them. I wondered how I could have done that, but it made me realize I need to approach my notes differently. I was approaching them too randomly. I should simply start from the beginning and go through the whole experience.

"He's helping me with some landscaping in the backyard with his brother and sister. How do you know Harris, are you friends of his?" she asked.

"I think he's already told you," Jeff answered.

She gave a confused look. Then, as the realization came, her face went white and tears came to her eyes. "You're the ones from the cliff?" she said with a trembling voice as she looked from Jeff to me and back to Jeff.

"Yes, we are," replied Jeff.

Her arms flew up and around Jeff's shoulders as the tears started flowing more freely. She then came to me and hugged me.

"Oh, I'm sorry, please come in." She opened the door and we walked in. "Oh, I'm his Aunt Iris, by the way."

Jeff introduced us in return.

"He'll be so happy to see you. So, so happy to see you." She led us to the back of the house and to a window with a view of the backyard. We could see Harris, his younger brother and sister alternating between yard work and horsing around with each other. The three of us stood at the window just watching them. It was a Norman Rockwell scene with a deserty twist. Harris was obviously someone his brother and sister adored and he adored them in return.

Iris, almost in a trance as she watched through the window, started talking. "Harris was fading fast and I had no idea what to do. I'd never been a mother, never even really wanted kids. Being an aunt was enough kid time for me. When their parents died in the car crash …" She turned and looked at us. "What else could I do? There was no one else."

Jeff wasn't saying anything so I tried to comfort her some. "It sounds like you did what needed to be done the best you could."

She smiled at me but it was more to thank me for trying to comfort her than for actually providing any comfort. She turned back to the window. "Harris and his father had a great relationship even though it was mostly around sports. After they died, Harris had to get a job to help me with bills. He lost his first string position on the football team and then we lost Harris."

She backed up and leaned against the wall but still looked outside. "One day he didn't show up for school, didn't show up for work, didn't answer his cell phone. I knew why." Iris was quiet for a minute, looking at the ground in thought. "I was able to hide it until I got his brother and sister to bed but after that I spent the evening crying." She looked at Jeff with tears in her eyes, "How's a person like me supposed to handle that?"

I watched Jeff's face respond to her question. This is just another thing that has amazed me about him since the day I met him. His face and eyes were probably more powerful and profound than his words. His look has an acceptance of your pain, an understanding of your pain, and a release of your pain.

Iris paused as she studied his face. Then she broke the gaze by looking down at the floor again. "It's not something you ever think about. When do you call the police? We've all seen the movies when they say a person has to be gone for twenty-four hours." She looked at us for understanding so I nodded. "Around two in the morning, my mind worked out that question. I took some breaths to quit crying, picked up the phone, and slowly started to dial hoping something would stop me between each number. I even looked up the number to the police station so I would have more numbers to dial instead of just 911." She looked up towards the front of the house as if she was recalling the event. "It worked. I stopped dialing when some lights shined in the window. I dropped the phone and ran to the door. Harris calmly walked up, hugged me, and said it was going to be okay." She looked back at us and then smiled. "I'm sorry. You didn't come here to hear me babble."

I wanted to respond but she turned to the back door too quickly. "Harris, someone's here to see you."

Harris playfully shoved his brother down and ran to the door before his brother could get up. He opened the door as he looked back with a smile to see if his brother was following him and then looked to see who was here. The smile vanished and he froze.

Jeff stayed where he was and gave Harris a warm smile. "Hello, Harris."

Slowly, as Harris processed what was happening, he smiled. "I never even got your names that night."

"I'm Jeff and this is Stanley."

"Jeff and Stanley." He paused and just looked at us. Then he repeated our names while looking at each of us as he said the name as if burning the image of the face and name together. "Jeff and Stanley." He looked over at his aunt with a smile and then back to us. "Everything's different now. Everything's going to be okay," Harris started. He looked at Jeff. "That book you gave me, *Man's Search for Meaning*. I read it straight through that night. It was, I don't know, amazing? That just doesn't seem to describe how much it spoke to me." He looked to me, his aunt, and then back to Jeff. "I have a future and there's meaning in that future. I have a brother and sister who need me." He looked at his aunt and paused. "I have an aunt who opened her house and life to us without ever questioning it."

Iris smiled at him with pride.

Their eyes locked on each other and I could see the profound connection the two had developed. Iris turned to us. "We can go to the living room. Seems better than standing here." We all turned and followed her.

Harris started talking as we walked. "I didn't even know a book could do that to someone. It was like a wall exploded in my brain." He held his fingertips to each side of his head and expanded them as he pulled his hands away from his head, "and another part of me, one I never knew was there, was open to explore. After I finished that book, I wondered if there were other walls other books would blow up." He sat on the couch next to his aunt and looked at us with a humorous grin. "I have a library card now and actually use it."

Jeff and I each took a seat in chairs facing the couch. After I was sat down I studied Harris' face. His statement about another part of his brain opening up was eerily close to what Deon had said.

Jeff said, "Walls exploding in your brain. I love that analogy. Now you're blowing up walls which were preventing your future."

Harris's eyes lit up as if Jeff hit a key point. "Yeah! Aunt Iris and I've been doing a lot of talking and planning and we're figuring out how to make it all work."

"I'm not at all surprised. What's the plan?" asked Jeff.

"I need … I want to go to college but I know we don't have the money. I've messed up my grades for the last couple of years so even if I get straight A's the rest of high school I won't be able to get an academic scholarship. But I can still get a sports scholarship if I can get back on first string. I've been talking to some scouts from some universities. Aunt Iris and I have worked out a plan so I can still work and go to all the practices."

"Any idea what you want to major in?" asked Jeff.

"Mr. Banner, my science teacher, has always tried to push me in science saying I was a natural."

Harris's brother, a boy of about ten years old, came into the room. "Are we done?"

Harris looked at him. "Matt, these are friends of mine, Jeff and Stanley".

We both said hello and I was going to say more but the boy turned back to Harris.

"So, we done? Julie and I wanna go play."

Harris nodded. "We need to get some more stone anyways. Can you put the tools away first?"

Matt didn't even answer and ran out of the room.

Harris turned to us and was trying to remember what he was saying.

Jeff helped his memory. "Mr. Banner?"

"Yeah! He always tried to get me to be interested in science but I'd always blown him off. My coaches said I had more of a shot at pro football than any kid they had ever worked with." He stopped and then held his hands out in front of him. "But since the day on the cliff I've been working at all of my classes in school, but Mr. Banner's science class has become, I don't know, like a place I should be, like a place I belong. I feel comfortable there. I like it there. I don't understand how I missed that before." He paused and then smiled. "Guess that wall in my head that exploded was stopping me. I've been talking to Mr. Banner about different degrees but I'm leaning towards quantum physics. I've been reading about it and can't seem to stop thinking about it. The future is locking up in there. I want to help unlock it."

At that point, I butted in, "So your plan is to go to college on a full sports scholarship and major in quantum physics?"

"Yeah, pretty wild isn't it? Most of the guys there are using college sports with the hopes of getting into the pros but I'm using sports to get an education. No one gets it. The university scouts are trying to talk me out of it. I've asked everyone the same question when they try to change my mind, 'Is the university there to get an education or to host a football team?' They have to think about it and then they have statements with a lot of 'buts' in them. They could care less about my education as long as I can help them win. A year ago, I would have thought they had my best interest in mind."

He was impressing me and making me believe he could do it.

Jeff said, "How would you like an internship at a place that can help you grow your knowledge in quantum physics? It'll help you meet your bills here and I can talk to your school to have it count towards a work-study program. You can work it all around your school and athletics schedule."

The expressions of Aunt Iris and Harris alternated several times between excitement and confusion. "How? There's nothing like that in town," Iris said.

"I have connections to a place that would love to have an enthusiastic young man like you. You could work remotely while you're in school. If your aunt is okay with it when you have breaks you can go there and work with some of the greatest minds and greatest people you'll ever meet. Just say the word and you have an internship."

Now their faces were just locked on the excitement as Harris' aunt moved closer to him on the couch and put her arm around his waist, holding him close as natural as any good mom would do. For a lady who was thrust into a situation she was not at all prepared for, she struck me as an outstanding woman. It was obvious she was doing her best to provide a family for her sister's kids.

Aunt Iris looked over at Harris with excitement yet was trying to make it look like it was up to him and would support his decision but Harris didn't need to think about it. "You could really do that? I wouldn't disappoint you if you could make that happen."

"I know you wouldn't. It's a done deal. Now, how about some dinner? My treat," offered Jeff.

"That sounds great," said Iris.

* * *

Jeff and I got in the Jetta and the four of them got in their car to follow us to Sally's restaurant.

"Internship? Can he do that from here?" I asked as we pulled away from the house.

"Yeah, it wouldn't be the first time." He looked towards me with excitement. "Once he said quantum physics, I knew we had a perfect place for him." He then waited with a goofy smile for the realization to come to me.

I cocked my eyes up in the air as I thought but it didn't take long for me to return the excited expression. "Grace! That's perfect. She would love to drag him into the depths of zero-point energy." I had one of those smiles that causes you to feel the stretch in your cheeks. "That's just too cool."

We were silent on the way to the restaurant. This was good because it gave me time to reflect on Harris and what he said. He talked about the book getting him to understand he had a future with meaning. Too clearly, I remembered the days before this trip where I couldn't see a future with meaning. Now, after this time with Jeff, I still wasn't sure about my future but I didn't have the constant fear eating away at my happiness. Maybe I'd been too busy and overwhelmed to think about it or maybe Harris, a high school boy, and I were traveling the same path of finding meaning in the future.

* * *

Pulling up to the restaurant was a surreal moment. It brought back some of the feelings I had when I first met Jeff.

"You know, our relationship was only a couple hours old the last time we were here, friend."

I ignored him for a moment while I looked out the window and tried to remember. The restaurant looked the same. Last time it was pretty full and from looking at the parking lot it looked to be crowded again. Without looking over at him I replied to his statement. "I don't think I like you any more than I liked you then. You've been nothing but a pain since the minute we met." I reached for my door handle and pushed. The dry desert heat over-powered all the work my air-conditioner had done.

Over the top of the car I heard, "Not even a little?"

This time I turned to him and smiled. "Not even a little."

Harris and his family parked on the other side of the parking lot in one of the few available spots. Near the door, we passed a motorcycle parking area with about ten bikes. Harris' group was still coming so I had some time to admire the bikes. I pointed to a burgundy and cream-colored one. "I like the new Indians. They're a nice looking bike."

Jeff went closer and squatted down to get a better look. "Yeah, It's a nice one. And the ..."

"You guys ready?" Harris interrupted.

Jeff rose from his squatting position. "Yep. Let's get some grub."

I placed my hand on the door handle to open it for everyone but then paused to read the papers taped to the door. It was a wedding announcement along with a note saying they were closing at 2:00 tomorrow and everyone had better be at the wedding.

I turned to Iris. "Do you know Sally Larsen or," I turned back to the door and read, "Theodore Reid?"

She shook her head. "No, I'm afraid I don't get out much. And now with the kids, it costs me so much." She turned to Jeff. "So, thanks for taking us. It's a real treat."

There was a small crowd just inside the door waiting to be seated.

A gray-haired waitress walked by right then and talked to the people waiting. "We have three or four tables leaving right now so we should get you seated shortly."

Iris was looking around. "Seems like a friendly place. Lots of smiles. Lots happening."

I saw about six waitresses rushing around trying to manage the crowd but none of them were Sally. I looked at Jeff. "Good, it looks like she isn't here today. It would be a shame for her to work the day before her wedding."

Jeff didn't respond but instead directed my eyes to Harris. He was just staring at one table. Looking in that direction, the memory of a high-school boy pulling a book out of his backpack and giving it to Jeff filled my mind. I remembered him saying he didn't need any of his books anymore. The way he was looking at the table made me wonder if that wasn't where he made the final plan. It also made me wonder if coming here for dinner was the right choice. I didn't even think about it until now.

A much younger waitress came up to us. "Okay, we are almost ready. How many in your group?"

"Six," I answered.

She pointed to the back-left corner. "We should be ready shortly."

Harris stopped her. "Any chance we can have that table? Looks like they are leaving." He pointed to the table he was staring at.

She turned, looked, and turned back. "Might be kind of tight for six." She looked at his brother and sister with a pleasant grin. "But I think we can pull a chair or two up and make it work."

Harris returned the same pleasant grin. "Thanks."

His Aunt Iris looked at the two tables and waited for the waitress to leave. "Sweetie, wouldn't the one in the corner be better?"

I was going to try to interject for Harris but, before I could, he looked at his aunt and calmly stated, "That table's where I made the worst choice of my life, and that table is where I met them and changed my life. Seems like a good place to get to know them more."

A young woman, maybe in her mid-twenties, with short black hair, came to our table with her order pad held out to take our orders. "Welcome everyone. Is this your first time here?"

"Second. He and I were here a couple of months ago." I answered.

Iris looked kind of sheepish. "Yes. It's my first time but it sounds like Harris has been here before. But I'm not as outgoing as him. Kind of a homebody."

The waitress let out a kind, short laugh. "I know how that is. I'll try to make it so you'll feel welcome to come back. We've been changing things up here over the last couple of months so we have some exciting things coming. We got a new cook who's shaking things up."

She seemed like a sweet girl. I smiled at her and inquired, "Shake it up? It was pretty good last time. That blackberry cobbler was amazing. A very nice woman named Sally waited on us. Is she around?" I thought the waitress was going to turn in circles, she was so excited.

"No! She's getting married tomorrow to the cook. And I'm the maid of honor! Never been in a wedding before. I'm jumping out of my skin, out of my mind excited. The dresses are just beautiful!"

I thought about telling her we were going but I didn't think we would ever get our orders if I did. She seemed more than happy to tell us about the wedding. "Sounds great. Too bad Sally isn't here but it sounds like she has a lot going on."

We chatted a bit more before she read off the specials and we placed our orders. As busy as the place was I was surprised at how fast the food got there. We enjoyed an outstanding dinner and got to know Harris and his family better. Matt and Julie, Harris's brother and sister, were great kids. For a young boy thrust into raising his siblings, he did a great balancing act of being a brother and being a parent. He was going to fit right in at Havens Research Institute.

Chapter 58

The next afternoon, in our suits, ready for the wedding, we pulled up to the church parking lot and tried to find a spot. I guess we should have gotten there sooner because the church parking lot was filled. We ended up taking one of the last spots in a parking lot a couple of blocks away.

I got out of the car and was hit with the dry heat. "We're going to be soaked in sweat by the time we get there. This sun is brutal."

A motorcycle made some of the car alarms beep near us as he slowly, but loudly, went by and then backed his bike into a spot too small for a car.

Jeff watched him. "At least we have AC. There's no escaping the heat on that."

We started down the parking lot towards the sidewalk and another bike caught my eye so I headed to it. "Hey, this is the Indian we saw at the restaurant."

Jeff walked up beside me and looked down at it. "Yeah. We get to enjoy it a second time, friend."

The heat from the blacktop was almost unbearable. I was getting anxious to get into the AC. Gently, I pulled Jeff's sleeve to let him know I was walking. We joined a group of people jaywalking across the street. They also seemed to be anxious to get out of the heat and weren't letting sidewalks slow them down. As we neared the church the crowd was getting bigger.

I was kind of irritated as it became obvious they were all heading to the church. Jeff and I were the only ones in suits. It seemed jeans, western shirts or biker leather were the proper attire.

I nudged Jeff. "Did you read the invitation? It seems everyone else got the memo about the dress code."

Jeff looked around at the crowd. "I swear it didn't say anything about that. Guess I should have asked Sally."

We walked through the front doors with the crowd and I sighed relief as I felt the AC blasting down in the church entryway. The foyer was a nice big area for gathering outside the sanctuary. The dark stone tile floors seemed to help give a coolness to the area.

Off to the left of the foyer, a bulletin board with a large emblem above it caught my attention. I tapped Jeff's shoulder and pointed.

"Ah, cool," he said and started walking that way.

Someone had painted '*Invite The Change*' above the bulletin board in big, elegant letters. The fact that it was painted seemed to give permanence to their commitment. On the board were pictures of people, I assumed from the congregation, at the schools working with children, at a jail looking at books with inmates, playing basketball with kids, and other community activities. There were lists of the plans they have created with other congregations and overall plans they wanted to achieve.

I looked at it approvingly. "This is great. Looks like they're taking it seriously here." I looked at Jeff. "Beth's church actually signed up. Hope they're taking it seriously."

He nodded and smiled. "Guess you'll find out soon. And if not, you can help them do that or take part with other groups."

I pushed the 'soon' part away. I wanted to get home but knew this time was important. I just nodded back and looked around more.

The size of the crowd surprised me. Sally didn't strike me as an overly social person. Maybe she was having a bad day when Jeff and I saw her. That day she looked like life had gotten the better of her. Maybe the guy she was marrying was the reason for the crowd.

Jeff and I worked our way past the groups of people mingling before they went into the sanctuary. Two men with leather vests with patches all over them were standing on either side of the doorway. Both watched as we approached. "Bride or groom?" the one to the left asked.

I smiled and replied, "Bride."

The one to the right was staring at us, making me mildly uncomfortable. I tried just looking into the sanctuary and avoiding his gaze. As our usher turned to have us follow him, the usher to the right said in a deep voice, "You're Jeff and Stanley, ain't you."

Jeff and I stopped and looked at him. "Yes?" I answered questioningly.

"Come on. Follow me." The man to the right turned and started down the aisle all the way to the front pew. "These are your seats."

As I sat down I nudged Jeff with my elbow. "You going to tell me what's happening. None of this fits with the woman who waited on us that day. And the front seats are usually reserved for family."

Jeff was looking at the altar. "They did a nice job decorating. The flower arrangements and candles are a masterful piece of work. And the lights shining through the chiffon arch."

I sighed. Getting an answer was pointless. Slouching back in the pew I looked up at the altar. "Yeah, it is nice. Guess I was expecting something more low-key. A lot went into this. For a girl who can't pay her electric bill, how did she afford this?"

"Glad she could though. It's a big day for her."

"Yeah, maybe she married into some money." I turned and scanned the attendees. "No, I don't think that's it. Oh, and the waitress said he's the cook at the restaurant. I doubt that pays very much." Then I looked at Jeff. "Or maybe she has an anonymous benefactor."

He was ignoring me and just admiring the décor.

After a while the music started, everyone quieted down and turned toward the back of the sanctuary. There was the young woman who I remembered seeing as a waitress yesterday, radiating excitement. She held her bouquet of light blue flowers in front of her. Her dress was a darker shade of blue than the flowers and hung to her knees. She looked very elegant and ready for the beauty of the event. But my head shot back as she removed her hand from the bouquet and took the elbow of a man in well-worn jeans and a leather vest. Then, one by one, an exquisitely attired woman took the elbow of a much less exquisitely attired man until four couples had passed us.

"This is interesting," I said to myself.

Then I saw our waitress from last night take her place in the back. She had said she was the bridesmaid. Another man in a leather vest and faded jeans came up to her and she took his arm. This time I knew the man, Zack.

The two started down the aisle, and when they got to us, Zack looked at us in surprise but then gave an approving nod. They passed us and then split to their assigned sides when they reached the front.

Quietly but with frustration, I whispered in Jeff's ear, "Zack? What's going on?"

He leaned his shoulder into me to push me away and then turned to the back. There was the groom, in an all-white tux with a white tie, starting down the aisle. In contrast to his groomsmen, he was clean-shaven, his neatly cut, dark blond hair was combed back and his smile pushed up his cheeks. I watched him slowly walk down the aisle as my mind worked overtime to place him. He reached the front row, turned and smiled at Jeff and me, and mouthed, "Thank you."

Once again, I was speechless. The long goatee was gone, the shaved head was replaced with a full head of hair and the look of death was replaced with a look of gratitude. Bear continued up to his place and waited. I looked up at the groomsmen and sure enough, now with the correct context, those were the guys from the bar that evening.

I looked at Jeff and he, with a devious look, simply said, "Surprise."

I clenched my teeth, elbowed him as hard as I could, and hissed, "I think I actually hate you now. Will you ever quit this mind-game crap?"

He looked at me and smiled. "Yes, I think I will, friend."

His statement caught me off guard. Jeff may like to play mind games, but his words were always of value. He turned to the back of the sanctuary again but I just looked at him. That statement carried more weight than the words would imply. To me, it translated to, "You have passed all my tests, Grasshopper. Your training is over."

A very cute flower girl, a year or two younger than Alice, so maybe four or five, started down the aisle dropping red rose petals in front of her. The traditional bride music came on and everyone stood as Sally started down the aisle with her hand through the elbow of, Nick, Bear's father. I thought that was odd, but regardless, she was radiating. They reached our row and both turned and smiled at us. Once at the front she extended both hands in front of her. Bear took a step forward and gently took hold of them. Their eyes locked on each other's and everybody's eyes locked on them.

Time went into slow-motion as I watched them look into each other's eyes. It was so hard to reconcile the Bear I remembered from the bar with the Bear smiling and looking into Sally's eyes with a profound respect and admiration.

The rest of the service went by in a blur as I simply watched the energy and connection flow between the two of them.

Without thinking, I found myself standing with the rest of the guests as Sally and Bear turned and started walking down the aisle. Sally released Bear's arm and quickly came over to Jeff and me. She gave us a quick hug and then went back to Bear. Arm and arm they retreated to the back of the sanctuary.

I looked at Jeff. "Wow. That was amazing. I mean, the way Bear looked at her. It was like," I tried to come up with a word but nothing came to mind. "I don't know. But it was something else."

Jeff nodded. "Yeah. I knew there would be something once I saw how Bear transformed in the bar. I knew Sally was the one to carry him through the rest of his transformation. In turn, he would be the one to help her find her strength. That's why I wrote her number in the book I gave him and told him to call her."

I nudged him and smiled. "I didn't picture you as a matchmaker."

He simply smiled at me.

I should have been more in awe of his ability to foresee what Bear and Sally could do for each other but instead, something else struck me. Jeff actually let me in on his plan without any games. He just told me straight up he had done this. Earlier he had said he was done with the mind games with me. This made it clear, Jeff and I were moving to a new stage in our relationship. My stomach knotted up because I knew the new stage wouldn't include him to any large degree.

People started exiting to the aisles so I pushed that out of my mind and slowly followed the crowd to a large multipurpose room for the reception and got in line to congratulate the bride and groom. It was sweet because I would catch Sally looking down the long line towards us and smile. She was checking to see how much longer it would take us to get there.

Jeff and I patiently waited in line but Sally was trying to not make it obvious she was impatient as she greeted the guests. I didn't want to look at her and make her more anxious so I watched the interesting variety of people and spent a little time admiring the wrapping job of the gifts on the gift table. Then a thought hit me. I turned to Jeff. "We didn't bring a gift. I didn't even think about it. Beth always handles that."

Jeff patted my shoulder. "I've got it covered."

I gave an appreciative nod. "Cool. Did we get them something nice?" I looked at the table. "And is it invisible? I didn't see you carrying anything in."

"I think they'll love it but we'll have to give it to them later."

"Great. What did we get them? I'd like to know how thoughtful I am."

Jeff paused, started to talk, and then paused again. Strangely, I knew what the issue was. We had developed a very deep-rooted communication pattern over the past couple of months. The pattern was, I would ask or say something and he would annoy me. It worked very well for us and was comfortable. But earlier Jeff implied it was time to move past that. I knew he was fighting the urge to give an elusive answer.

I held up my hand. "No, in fact, I want to be surprised at my thoughtfulness also." I rubbed my hands together. "I can't wait to see what we got them."

Jeff put his arm around me and gave me a one-armed hug. "Thanks, friend. I'll even give you the honor of inviting them. See if they will meet us tonight."

I smiled. "Seems fair. I should do my part."

When we finally got there, Sally let out a quiet squeal of excitement as she wrapped her arms around both of us and whispered repeatedly, "Thank you!! Thank you!!" in our ears. She reached down and picked up the flower girl and brushed her blond hair to the side out of her eyes. "Hope, these are the men who brought us Teddy."

Hope smiled and excitedly held out her arms for a hug. "Thanks for bringing me my Teddy bear."

Jeff bent in to receive the hug and I held back a laugh. Teddy Bear was the one who knocked the crap out of Jeff. But I didn't get to reflect on that for long because my hug was next.

Hope whispered in my ear, "Mommy smiles now. Thank you."

I had no idea how to respond so I just enjoyed the hug and smiled at her when she released me. Then a massive hand landed on my shoulder and I was effortlessly pulled into Bear's chest. "Well Superman, looks like you saved the day." His arms went around me and, as my rib cage threatened to collapse, I couldn't help but wonder how Jeff survived that day. I reached around to return the hug but my hands patted his shoulder blades.

Bear released me from the hug and looked down the line at the people waiting, then back at Jeff and me. "Sally and I would love it if we could spend some time with you later. Are you guys going to be around?"

Sally added, "Nothing big. Both Teddy and I talked, and it seems our first meeting with you two was not the best. We wanted to get to know you a little and thank you."

I nodded and then took up my part of the wedding gift. "That would be great, perfect in fact. We have a gift for you but we need to meet with you. We can do that then."

Bear looked over at Sally excitedly. "Can we call you when things settle down?"

Jeff said, "Sally has my number. We'll be ready when you are."

That was settled so we quickly moved out of the way so the other guests could greet them.

I gave Jeff a soft punch. "Sally has *my* number."

He laughed. "Potato – Potahto."

Chapter 59

It was a little after six o'clock when my phone rang. I was sitting in my hotel bed writing in my notebook about the wedding. I hadn't gotten too far because Jeff and I had just gotten back from a simple fast food dinner. Jeff had told me to have them meet us at the hotel so I gave them the address and wrote for a few more minutes before going to Jeff's room.

The sun was low enough in the sky that the two-story hotel gave us shade as we waited. It had cooled to the low 80's so, with the shade it wasn't bad. I leaned against the Jetta watching the highway traffic pass and wondered what our gift was. This wasn't unusual for me. When Beth and I went to weddings I never knew what gift we were giving.

We didn't have to wait too long before a mid-nineties Civic came our direction. Sally was driving, Bear was wedged in the passenger seat, and Bear's dad, Nick, was in the back with Hope. Sally pulled up behind the Jetta and rolled down her window.

Jeff lowered himself to eye level. "Can you follow us?"

"Sure," Sally said.

"Great." Jeff stood and held out his hand for the keys so I tossed them to him. Jeff pulled out of the hotel and on to the service road with Sally trailing close behind. He then went down the highway a couple of miles before exiting and navigating into a residential area. The houses here were not packed as tight as Iris and Harris' neighborhood. There was plenty of open area with sand and desert brush filling the lots between the houses. He pulled into the crushed stone driveway of a house at the very eastern part of a sparsely populated neighborhood and shut off the car.

I looked at the house through the windshield. It was an impressive house. It wasn't huge but the design made you look at it and study it. There was a large covered front porch that said, "come sit here and have a lemon-aid with me and talk." The metal roof had some interesting changes in its plains and pitches which added an architectural beauty not seen on most houses. Much like Iris' house, the landscaping drew from the natural surroundings, adding to their beauty instead of fighting with the desert.

I turned from the windshield and looked at Jeff. "Really?"

He smiled and shrugged. "Sort of." Then he turned and pulled a folder out of his backpack in the back seat.

We both exited the car and watched Sally and her crew get out with curious looks.

Jeff walked up to their Civic. "Let me do some explaining before you get too excited. This is a different type of wedding present. Let's call it a wedding opportunity instead." He turned and motioned them to follow him. "Let me explain before we look around. I want you to understand before we go any further."

This just added to their confusion, and in fact, added to mine. Jeff started walking towards the inviting front porch while Sally and Bear waited for Nick to finish getting Hope out of the car.

I ran and caught up with Jeff. Quietly I said, "Please tell me we're bringing them here to see the waffle iron," I did air quotes, "'*we*' bought them. I can split the cost of that with you, but I can't split the cost of a house."

Jeff stuck out his lower lip and nodded thoughtfully. "Waffle iron? That would've been a great gift, friend. Wish we would've talked before. But it's too late now. This will have to do."

We climbed the three stairs to the large covered porch. There was a table with four chairs around it towards the center of the porch and, to the far left, was an outdoor couch and chairs. It was like a living room in the outdoor shade. I turned and looked at Sally and her crew walking this way with the sun getting lower in the sky behind them. There was an unobstructed view of the desert. "Man, what a great place to watch the sunset."

Jeff turned. "Yeah, I could see relaxing with some friends and family and watching that every evening." He turned and pulled out one of the four chairs from the porch table and sat down.

I had expected him to go inside to take advantage of the air condition but he didn't. He motioned for me to sit in one of the other chairs beside him and waited for the four from the Civic to get here.

Jeff laid the folder on the table and the cover lifted open by a gentle breeze. Jeff closed it and placed his hand over the folder to prevent the paper from blowing away.

The air had cooled down a few degrees from the day's high and the breeze made the porch a pleasant place to sit.

Bear and Sally climbed up the stairs and looked around questioningly. Jeff held his hand out toward the two remaining chairs at the table so they joined us. Nick and Hope made themselves at home on the other side of the porch on the comfortable looking couch. I smiled as I watched Hope climb on Nick's lap and then place her hands on each side of his face to playfully contort his cheeks into different shapes. Nick may have failed as a father but he wasn't missing a beat as a grandfather. I turned back from watching that to see the other three smiling as they watched the same show.

Jeff interrupted the moment. "As I said, this is a different kind of wedding present. You don't have to take it if you don't want to. Stanley and I will get you the waffle iron we thought about instead."

Bear looked at Jeff without a smile and with a gruff voice asked, "What kind of waffle iron? Sally and I were looking at some and we wouldn't just want any old waffle iron."

I gave an internal smile. Who would have guessed Bear had a sense of humor? Then I looked at Jeff. "See! I told you. A waffle iron was a sure thing."

Jeff sighed and played right along with us. "I should have listened. But would you humor me and see what my idea is?"

Bear turned and gave Sally a serious look. "What do ya' think, baby? You know how bad we were looking forward to a lifetime of waffles in the morning."

Sally reached out and placed her hand on Bear's massive hand. "Honey, let's at least listen to him. And if we don't like it, he said we could trade."

Bear gave her a nod and turned to Jeff. "You have a tough sell, but we'll listen."

Jeff broke the moment with the first smile. "That's all I ask." He opened the folder and handed a package of papers to them. "It's all explained in these, but in essence, this is an equity-only payment plan. There's a suggested monthly payment, if you can pay it, that goes to the equity. If you can't pay it some months, then all that happens is you don't pay down the equity those months. When or if you decide for a life change, you sell, pay off the balance then the equity is yours."

Both Bear and Sally looked at Jeff and then each other as they processed what Jeff was saying. Then Sally started reading. After about five minutes Sally looked at Jeff. "That payment seems low and also the total price seems low."

Jeff nodded. "Yeah, and there's a good reason for that. You see, where Stanley and I work, they're testing a lot of different building materials and techniques. We were able to get a lot of that here at a very low cost to test it in the desert. And when I say 'test', I don't mean there's any risk to you. We just want to monitor and get some data."

Bear gave Jeff a questioning look. "Testing? What are you testing?"

Jeff held out his index finger towards Bear. "There's the question I'm excited about. You can finish reading those later. You don't have to decide today." Jeff stood and then looked around. "I'm not sure where to start." He made a motion towards the door but then stopped. "Oh, while we are here let me start with that. Designing for the desert is different. We have architects working with others to design for that. The obvious reason for a porch this big is for shade. It keeps the sun off the walls and windows. The other side of the house has just as big of a porch. But the bigger reason is to get the surface area for water collection. This area only gets about six inches of rain a year. So, with the increase of surface area, we can capture more water to store in underground tanks."

Nick walked over to us carrying Hope.

Bear was looking up at the roof. "How much water? I mean, it can't be that much."

Jeff nodded. "Data and testing, remember. That's why you're getting this cheap."

Sally looked a little worried. "What happens if it isn't enough? Do we still have city water?"

Jeff shook his head. "Barstow could shut everything down tomorrow and this house would just keep humming along. As far as it being enough water, we think so. The water system is not conventional. For example, when you take a shower, nothing comes out until the water is at the right temperature. Then that water goes into a gray water system that's used for flushing toilets and other functions where you don't need potable water." He shrugged. "And if it happens to not be enough water, you get a truck to come put some in your tanks."

She smiled. "Guess that sounds easy enough."

Jeff walked over and placed his hand on the wall. The wall and trim were painted in tans and browns which accented the natural colors of the desert. "Most of the walls are magnesium oxide board instead of your typical drywall interior and cement board exterior. That makes them fireproof, insect-proof, mold-proof, etc." He walked to the front door. "With other walls in the house, we created thermal mass to help regulate the interior temperatures."

Bear placed his hand on the wall and examined it but then asked a totally different question. "What about power? You said the city could shut down so that would mean power too."

Jeff had just grabbed the door handle but let go and walked off the porch. We all joined him and looked at the roof where he was looking. "Photovoltaic is progressing fast. The whole roof is coated with a membrane that produces an impressive amount of electricity. And it just looks like a roof."

Bear looked impressed as he scanned the roof. "No panels? I always hated those. They just look out of place." He then looked back at Jeff. "So, we're set during the day. What about night?"

Jeff patted my shoulder. "I'll let Stanley tell about this. He's the expert here." Jeff turned to his right and started walking.

I was confused until we turned the corner and felt a jolt of excitement. I walked up and reverently placed my hand on the tan containment vessel of a flywheel. I had worked on these for the past two months in the lab, but the excitement of seeing one being used caused shivers.

My thoughts were interrupted when Jeff said, "Well, you going to just admire it or tell the newlyweds what it is?"

Mildly embarrassed I turned towards them. "Sorry, I've just never seen one of these outside the lab. This is a flywheel and will store enough power to run the house for days. Between this and the solar membrane, you'll never be out of power."

Sally and Bear looked on and nodded. I don't think it was anywhere near as special of a moment for them as it was for me.

I continued. "No more chemical batteries. No more grid being used as the backup storage of excess power. Once these flywheels are out there, energy independence can start being a reality."

I looked at them hoping they would see the significance but they only politely smiled back with no real understanding of what this meant. Then I looked at Jeff. His eyes locked on mine and returned my excitement. He then turned and started back to the front of the house.

Everyone was quiet until, climbing the porch stairs, Sally said, "So we won't have a water bill or an electric bill?"

Jeff turned, and with a knowing look said, "No. You will never have an electric bill."

Sally paused and looked at Jeff. I knew exactly what she was thinking. The tip Jeff left her two months ago was the amount she needed to keep her electricity turned on. She would never be stressed about that again. She walked up and gave him a long hug.

The six of us toured the rest of the house. We saw much of the technology I had seen from the building technologies division of HRI. It was masterfully interwoven throughout the house. But like the flywheel, it didn't carry the same significance to them as it did to me. To them, they had a nice house they could afford and would never pay utilities again.

Sally put her arm around Teddy. "I think we may have to buy our own waffle iron."

As Teddy nodded in agreement I was struck with the fact that Sally decided without even confirming with Teddy. Granted, there was no real choice to make, but still, she had a strength she didn't have two months ago. The Sally from two months ago would have looked towards Teddy to do the talking and stayed in the background. In contrast, the Bear of two months ago would have made sure she stayed in the background. But Teddy let her strength flower.

We went back out to the patio table and Nick walked out into the yard to explore with Hope. The new couple read the documents and signed them. Jeff held out his hand with a set of keys. The deal was done.

Sally reached out and took the keys thoughtfully. Once they were in her hand she held them near her waist looking at them. A tear fell into her hand. Her other hand reached up and wiped her eyes. She sniffed and looked up to Jeff. "You gave me a book that day, *A Tree Grows in Brooklyn*. Just some book some kid had in his backpack. I hadn't read a book in years." Her hand wiped her eyes again. "You said a tree was growing in Barstow. I didn't know what that meant. I started reading it simply because you asked me to. I figured I owed you for the money. I finished and still didn't know what you meant. Then I get a phone call from a guy saying someone gave him a book and had told him to call my number. He didn't even know who he was calling."

Teddy laughed. "You can't imagine hearing that sweet voice and trying to figure out who this nut was having me call. Just like Sally did, I read *Jubel Sackett*, the book you gave me, just because you said to. Guess it was a good story and all, but nothing came to mind when I finished. I made that phone call and Sally and I decided we should at least meet. There must be a reason you had me call her. I was so nervous mostly because I don't normally just go meet everyday people. Criminals and outlaw bikers I know how to talk to. You just have to scare them more than they scare you. I was good at that. But to just go meet a waitress, with no idea of what I was meeting her for? I wasn't sure how to act. Jubel, the character from the book, was the quiet one but treated people with respect. I played that part when I met her. Sat and listened to her like what she was saying was important."

She reached out and took his hand. "I don't think anyone had ever listened to me before. Here was this monster looking of a man looking at me, listening to me like I was someone. That's when I understood the book and a tree started growing in Barstow."

Teddy looked away from her and to us. "And I found the Jubel personality I was trying on was a pretty good fit for me. Except, I'm not the quiet one like him, but the rest wasn't as much work as being angry. Being with Sally was relaxing and easy. With her, I didn't feel like I had to maintain my image."

They were both quiet for a minute as they looked at Jeff. Then Sally said, "How did you know we would do that to each other? How could you have possibly known?"

I turned to Jeff eagerly waiting to see how he'd answer this question.

He looked at each of them in turn. "Right here, right this minute, is not the time to answer that question. But please know the answer is coming and there is a reason you are together."

I was disappointed in the answer but they both nodded understandingly. Sally patted Teddy's hand. "You know where to find us when the time is right." She was about to say more but Hope had finished her exploring and was at her mother's side.

Jeff stood. "I think it is time for all of you to acquaint yourself with your new house."

We said our goodbyes and my final hug was with Hope before I handed her to Bear. The crushed stone crunched quietly under our feet as Jeff and I walked to the Jetta. I opened the passenger door and started to get in. I stopped when I heard Bear calling out.

"Oh! In all the excitement I almost forgot. Is there any chance you guys would go to church with us tomorrow morning? It's the same place we had the wedding."

Jeff looked at me over the top of the car. "It's up to you."

I flashed back to Jeff asking me to go to church with him in Bethlehem. Do you tell the messiah, or whatever he is, you don't want to go to church with him? There was still time to make it to Bakersfield tonight but this is about what I expected when I told Beth we would be home tomorrow. I looked at the family on the porch. "Would love to. We'll see you there."

We waved and got in the car. As I backed out I took a verbal jab at Jeff. "You totally punted. They asked you how you did what you did and you punted."

Jeff shook his head. "Not really. It wasn't the time. I was hoping to stop for some ice cream before we went to the hotel. If I said something like," he deepened his voice, "'I'm the new Messiah with a message from God.' We would have never got to the ice cream place before it closed."

"So, the message from God was usurped by ice cream?"

"Yeah? You're not okay with that?"

I raised my shoulder towards my ear. "Guess it depends on the ice cream."

He nodded. "See, you get it. Most people don't and they ask too many questions. Offer you pizza or ice cream and everything's cool. Besides, once the book's out there'll be a lot less explaining to do. People will already have a bunch of the answers so I won't have to explain as much."

Unconvinced, I nodded and simply said, "I see."

Chapter 60

In the morning, we made our way to the church where the newlyweds had their ceremony. Bear had requested we come to the adult Sunday school class so we made sure we were there in plenty of time. We found him waiting excitedly for us in front of the church with two Bibles under his arm, Hope in his other arm, and his dad, Nick, standing beside him.

When we got closer, Hope held out her arms so I could take her.

Bear said, "She wanted to see you guys before her Sunday school class." Proudly he added, "Sally's teaching it. She's there right now getting ready for her class." He reached out and took Hope from me and set her on the ground. "Grandpa will walk you to class now." He then kissed her as Nick took her hand.

Hope kissed him back and said, "Love you, Teddy," and then left with Nick.

As I watched Hope walking away holding Nick's hand, it brought back memories of either my dad or Beth's dad walking with Alice, reaching up, holding their hand. I don't know why, but those types of memories seem to hold a special place in my mind. Noticing Jeff and Bear watch with smiles made me think I wasn't the only one with that special place in my mind.

It wasn't until Nick and Hope rounded the corner that Jeff inquired, "So, Bear or Teddy?"

Bear turned his gaze, from where it was focused, to Jeff. He shrugged. "I don't know. Seems like if I say not to call me Bear I'd be trying to deny my past. But I was that person and I own what that person did. I'm not going to live in regret or denial of that.

Bear got me standing right here with a princess telling me she loves me, a dad willing to be part of my life, and a woman who gives me more strength than I ever knew I had." He put his hands in his pockets and looked down, thinking. "Bear taught me a lot in some very painful ways." He looked back up. "Yet, Teddy is the person born out of all that and the one who will try to right the wrongs caused by Bear. So, either one is fine. Guess it depends on who you see me as now."

Jeff reached up and put his hand on the man's shoulder. "Well Teddy, let's get out of this heat." We turned to go and Jeff, as if an afterthought said, "Oh, and Teddy, we have shared some amazing experiences. Would you do me a favor and let those be our experiences?"

Teddy was watching Jeff as he spoke but then looked forward as we walked. He was turning over a lot in his mind. "I don't know who you are or your purpose. Guess I kind of figured you'd clue this old biker in when it was he needed to know." He looked at me and then back to Jeff. "And you two have given me more than a man can normally handle, as far as change. So right now, I just need the support of a couple of good friends. That's what you are to me. But when you need me, nothing will get in my way."

"Thanks, friend."

Once inside the adult's classroom, Teddy placed his Bibles on a white plastic folding table and started eagerly introducing 'his good friends' to the dozen or so men and women of the class. We made our way around the rectangle formed from the tables, meeting the class, until it was time for Sunday school to start. At that time, Teddy introduced us to the teacher, Oswald, who had just walked in. It was so strange seeing this monster size of a man, an ex-drug dealer, and who knew what other heinous crimes could be pinned on his past, sitting zestfully on the edge of his white folding chair waiting for Sunday school to begin.

Oswald appeared to be in his mid-forties, with a full head of black hair and a peaceful face. He looked in control yet the type of guy you could just go talk to. The class was starting to cover the book of Matthew and Oswald started the class with, "I sure hope everyone studied this during the week. I'm not here to read it to you. I'm here to grow with you so I better be challenged."

The first part was the genealogy of Jesus, and Teddy followed along intently, referring to some handwritten notes he had. I looked down at the Bibles he had sitting on the table in front of him and one seemed to be a reference Bible with Greek and Hebrew.

I questioningly looked over at Jeff to which he replied, "He's been studying pretty much non-stop and the stupid brute is far from stupid. Just watch."

The next part of Matthew was about the birth of Jesus and the class leader read as Teddy followed along in his Bible. "The virgin will be with child and will give birth to a son, and they will call him Immanuel."

Teddy looked at his notes and then his hand went up. "I was looking at this section during the week. And, as you know, I don't have much background in this area so I've been doing some catch-up. The virgin birth is interesting so I was reading more about it. The Greek word used is *parthénos* and can mean virgin or young maiden. One source I looked at said this verse in Matthew is in reference to the prophecy in Isaiah and that uses the Hebrew word *almah*. The word *almah* can translate to an unmarried woman. In fact, the English word 'virgin' in some dictionaries is also given the meaning unmarried woman. So, is there a chance our idea of virgin is not the best way to interpret this?"

Jeff leaned over to me, "Non-stop."

What happened next was just as interesting as seeing the biker talk about Greek and Hebrew translations. Oswald calmly responded with a smile and then started reading his own Bible out loud in Greek. "I'm not sure about that Teddy but I'm not saying you're wrong, I'm saying I don't know. Anybody?"

A woman in her fifties, sitting directly across from me in the rectangle, replied, "I'm so glad you brought that up. It has always bothered me. I've heard different things over the years, like the virgin birth was patterned from older religions or something to do with Cesar at the time, but I never explored it. I would love to look into that more."

"Hogwash!" said a man to the right of Jeff. "What would be the point of it? Sounds like someone trying to bring in questions where questions aren't needed. And, even if it ended up being true, what changes? Do we stop feeding the hungry, clothing the poor, stop loving our neighbor? Isn't that the heart of why we're Christians?"

Teddy, leaned forward to look past Jeff and me, to see the man who just spoke. "Man, I love what you bring to this class. I totally agree with that. I just am new to this and have lots of questions. Humor me?"

The man leaned past Jeff and studied Teddy. "Consider yourself humored. I've been wrong too many times. Don't see the harm in exploring with a man who wants to grow."

Oswald had a big smile. "Can't tell you how much I love this. We have some very ingrained ideologies in Christianity that should be examined but examining them may, in itself, threaten what we have been told our whole lives is the absolute truth. How do we deal with that? Do we take what we've been told our whole life as the absolute truth or do we question it? I think to answer that question, all we have to do is look at what Jesus did in his life. He turned many of the beliefs of his time upside down. I think if Jesus was sitting here right now he would be telling us to question, learn and grow."

I couldn't help but look at Jeff after Oswald's comment.

Jeff said, "I think you're right about that."

Oswald looked at Jeff and smiled, not even knowing what just happened. "Thank you. Jeff, it was, right?"

Jeff nodded.

Oswald continued, "I don't think we can answer that today. Anyone interested in researching and reporting what you find out next class? That would make an interesting discussion."

Teddy, the other two who commented, and a couple of others volunteered.

Oswald added, "Don't forget to include your sources. I want to see where the information is coming from."

A shiver of excitement ran down my spine. This would have never happened in Beth's church. There, Sunday school seemed purely about indoctrination. There was no questioning going on. If church was like this, I would be interested in going instead of only supporting Beth.

Oswald ended the class by saying, "And you know what I always say."

There was a unison reply from the class, "Love over Law and Do over Dogma."

Oswald smiled and replied, "You got it, now do it."

* * *

When Sunday school was over Teddy headed back to the kid's classes as Hope came running out the door and flew into his arms and he swung her around.

Nick walked out of the door much more calmly than Hope and was followed by Sally. Nick looked at us. "Hope you didn't miss me. I decided to stay in Hope's class with Sally. Figured it was more at my level."

Teddy just gave his father a smile.

The six of us went to our seats and Hope took what seemed to be her natural spot on Teddy's lap. The service started with prayer, songs, and announcements.

For the announcements, an older woman came to the podium with a notebook and took some time to find her place in it. She went through the typical list you would expect from a church with upcoming meetings, prays for the sick, and celebrations. For the celebrations, she looked out at Sally and Teddy and remarked on what a beautiful wedding it was. Then she turned the page of the notebook and scanned it. She smiled and looked out. "There's a lot here. We had our community member meeting earlier this week and got some great ideas on what they feel needs to happen. I'll try to be quick. Let's see." She scanned again. "Well, I guess I won't read all the *Invite The Change* committee meetings. They're listed on the board out front and if you're on one of the committees then you probably already know when your meetings are. Mainly, we're looking for people with some different skills." She pointed at her notes. "Here's one I was looking at but my grandkids won't let me. We need some skaters to hang out at the skate park. That isn't a good one for me ... my ollie has left me." She paused and looked up. "It's a skater joke."

There was a laugh in the congregation at the thought of a gray-haired grandma skating at the skate park.

She continued, "So I'll continue tutoring at the girl's shelter. If you don't have much time we always need people to go to the schools and read. We have slots for that on the sign-up sheet." She continued, but ended with, "We have many people with many different talents. This is a much-needed program, so find a way to get involved and help build a connected community. I just love how this program revolves around people from the communities needing help, reaching out and asking, inviting change. Then people in communities who want to help, their job is to listen and work with that community. What I've seen since we started is we don't have separate communities. They are all growing together, becoming connected, becoming one community." She picked up her notebook and looked out. "I'd better go now before I turn this into a sermon."

The congregation laughed as I grabbed a piece of paper and pencil from the holder in the back of the pew and wrote, 'connected'. There was Derrick's word again. I looked at the word and wondered about my future with it. But then wondered about my past with it. Had I ever really connected with anything or was I just haphazardly moving through life? I put a question mark after the word. My time of reflection was cut short when Oswald came to the pulpit. I was excited about this. He wasn't introduced as the minister so this was a pleasant surprise.

He placed his hands on either side of the podium and leaned forward. "Most of the problems we face today aren't new. As Solomon said in Ecclesiastes, 'There is nothing new under the sun.' Ancient stories of all cultures and all religions deal with exactly the same human conditions we still battle. Greed, envy, fear, hate, pride, regret, vengeance, just to name a handful, have plagued humanity since the beginning of humanity. The message of most, maybe all, religions is counter to those. The message of love, forgiveness, acceptance, peace, unity has echoed from religious text after religious text for thousands of years, yet we still fight for those words to become the way of life instead of the exception." Oswald backed up from the podium and crossed to the left of the pulpit. "Let's look at the story of Joseph who was sold into slavery by his jealous brothers. As we all know, Joseph rose to become one of the most powerful people in Egypt. And when his brothers come to him, not knowing it was their brother, how does he respond? How would you have responded? Anger and regret are very expensive. They *will* cost you the rest of your life. Happiness has no home in a heart focused on anger, revenge, or regret. We can see that in the story of Joseph. Forgiveness buys you a future and it doesn't require a payment plan."

This caused me to think of Teddy and his father. I looked over and saw Teddy's arm resting across his father's shoulder as they both listened intently. Sally was holding Teddy's other hand. I don't think Teddy's mind was on how he had forgiven his dad. As

Oswald had said, there wasn't a payment plan. Teddy and Nick paid the price and moved on.

Oswald moved to the right side of the pulpit. "Now, let's look at this story a different way. What if Joseph's brothers did not sell him into slavery? He was favored by his father. He may have inherited his father's domain and had dominion over his brothers. He might have had material goods but not the love and respect of his brothers. That envy would have lived on to his dying day. As I see it, that would have been a best-case scenario for Joseph. But because he was sold by his brothers, he became one of the most powerful men in Egypt. He was able to help many people. He won the love and respect of a nation. And then, on top of that, because he was able to forgive, he won the love and respect of his brothers."

This made me shiver. It was exactly what Bear was saying in front of the church. Bear, or Teddy, was living the sermon. I turned to Jeff, and with more respect for the phrase he used the first day I met him, I echoed, "It's all part of the experience."

He smiled and nodded.

I underlined the word *forgiveness* on the sheet of paper.

Oswald moved back to the podium. "There's a couple of things I want you to take away from this. One, the things which go wrong in life may be the best things that ever happen to you. Two, the same message has been taught for many thousands of years. Maybe we can be the first generation to fully realize the message and truly live it."

Chapter 61

Church ended and we all started filing out. Jeff put his arm around my shoulder. "Do you want to see if they want to get something to eat or do you just want to get on the road?"

I looked at him with a blank expression. I was so ready to get home but I had resolved my time with Jeff to just be my time with him. So, how was I supposed to answer that? I opened my mouth but didn't know what to say.

Jeff started before I could get any words to come out. "You know, I really have a taste for a bacon double cheeseburger and a malt. Why don't we just get something and go?"

I smiled. "Onion rings?"

His head moved approvingly. "I think you and I are finally getting on the same wavelength. Let's get going."

Once outside we said our sad goodbyes to the new family. They said they were looking forward to cooking their first lunch in the new house. So, I felt better about not going to lunch with them.

On the way to the car, I called Beth to let her know we would be home in a few hours and she squealed in excitement. After that, I picked up my pace to the car with Jeff trailing behind me. Within fifteen minutes we were through the drive-thru and on the road. Within another fifteen minutes, Jeff was into his normal state with his seat reclined a little and reading.

For me, on the other hand, this part of my journey dredged up a wealth of polar emotions. Today, I was finally going to be home. I was so excited to see my family after my extended absence. But, I was also leaving something, which during that absence, had driven itself so deeply into my psyche, I was afraid to leave it. I'd witnessed and learned so much. With Jeff there and the support of everyone at the Institute, even though it was an overwhelming experience, I was able to thrive. Now I was leaving the support and understanding. That was the big fear which I always pushed out of my mind. Once home, would Beth support me? So far, I had no reason to doubt she would but Jeff's refusal to answer my question haunted me. This trip was an awakening for me. My vertical growth was just starting. If Beth was not on that path with me, would that try our relationship past its boundaries? She only heard about it from me, she hadn't experienced it.

I tried to redirect my fear away from Beth, back to being without Jeff to figure out what was next. I needed to find another job, but how could I ever walk into another place and be happy after experiencing the Institute? I wasn't a strong enough person to walk into a place and start making changes and improving the place. When Grace leaves the Institute, where ever she ends up isn't going to know what hit them because she has the strength to do that. I'm not that type of person. I've been a technical writer for so long I didn't know what else I could even do. I had to make a career change but was drawing a total blank as to what that could be. Then my mind drifted back to Jeff's comments on Deon's struggle and how I should keep that in mind. Was he warning me that Beth and I were in trouble? I should've been excited to finally be coming home, but as we got closer, the reality of my future started dominating my thoughts.

Jeff lowered his book and stared out the windshield. I watched him out of the corner of my eye knowing this was in preparation to say something. He left me to contemplate what it might be for about half a minute before turning his head towards me. "I'm asking absolutely nothing of you when our paths separate."

Giving my own dramatic pause, I thought about his statement before turning my head slightly towards him. "I don't buy that. You took me on this strange journey for a reason. You need me to do something. You've even told me you need me to do something for you but refuse to tell me what that is."

"What I need you to do is be Stanley. That's it," he said.

That caused me to smile. "It's funny. When I told Beth you were coming she got nervous. After all the stories I've told her, I can understand. But I also know you and guess what I told her?"

Playfully, he held up his hands beside him and shrugged. "I haven't the faintest."

"Really? Not the faintest?" I said with a grin. "Well, I told her to just be Beth."

He looked at me approvingly. "That's wise advice and sounds vaguely familiar. It's …"

I interrupted him. "It's easy advice to give but hard to take. What does, 'be Stanley' mean? It may not have dawned on you, but I was Stanley before I pulled up to the stoplight and picked you up."

"Yes, you were, and because you were Stanley then and because you are Stanley now, you will do what I need you to do just because you are Stanley," he answered with no real comfort to me.

My look turned from playful to mildly irritated. "So just keep wondering why I can't get anywhere in my career, wonder why I can't pay my bills, wondering why I can't afford to take my family on vacations, wondering why I sit in church wanting to believe but not being able to, wondering why I can't keep my garage clean, wondering if I'm a good enough father and husband, wondering what I want to be if I ever grow up?" After all of that fell out of my mouth my expression changed from mildly irritated to slightly angry. "Is that your plan? If so, your plan sucks."

A rare thing happened. The smile left his face and in a serious voice he asked, "Is that still how you see yourself?" Before I could respond he held up his hand to stop me. "I know your time with me has been stressful. It's a lot to take in. So, I'm going to give you a break and going to tell you something I want you to do for me."

Now I went from angry to shocked. "Really? Hold on." There was a wide deserty shoulder to my right, so I pulled about twenty feet from the highway and shut off the car. Then I reached behind the seat to get my notebook. "Remember, you said there would be no more mind games. Okay. I'm ready, oh Great One. What is it you request of me?"

He looked at me a little worried. "I don't think pulling over and the notebook are needed. I think you're going to be disappointed."

I shook my head and stopped him. "No, you're doing it all wrong. The delivery has to be good. This is a big moment and requires the right voice and such. You know, a deep, booming voice starting with something like, 'I, the great and powerful Jeff do command'." I stopped and shook my head. "You know, 'Jeff' isn't a good name for this sort of thing. Guess that's why Oz took that name. But it's the best we have for now so just work with it." I undid my seatbelt so I could turn and watch him better.

He looked at me questioningly. "You sure? I'm afraid you're setting us up for failure."

Moving my hand in front of me in a small circle I said, "No, no, this is good. I'm ready." I opened my notebook and took out my pen.

He shrugged. "Okay. I usually save that voice for very important and dramatic times." He cleared his throat and opened his mouth.

From inside my head, from inside my bones, from every air molecule around me, space itself became words and they said, "I, the great and powerful Jeff, that was your phrasing by the way, not mine, do command that Stanley Whitmore take six or so months off to relax and regroup. Take more time if you feel like it. Take a family vacation and if you need some extra cash during that time, just let me know."

In a futile attempt to escape the omnipresent words I grabbed my door handle but because I had my back on the door I fell out, rolled on the hard-packed sand, and covered my ears. The words didn't hurt but I was in no way ready for words consuming my whole being and space around me. The effect was overwhelming.

But then there was an overwhelming silence. I took my hands away from my ears and there was the wind of a car on the highway and some background desert life sounds. It might have been the ants digging in the sand. The engine crackled from metals changing temperatures. But these were just simple sound waves making my eardrums move and sending signals to my brain. It wasn't the sound of the infinity of space speaking to me.

Then, an old, familiar, and safe sound wave vibrated my eardrums. "It was a bit much, wasn't it?"

Sharply I turned my head towards the sound waves and saw Jeff coming around the car towards me. He squatted down to get more to my level and just looked at me with a rare worried look.

The words which came out of my mouth were not the words I expected. "The whole 'great and powerful Jeff' thing takes away from the effect. It comes across as arrogant. Let's come up with something better."

I felt better seeing the worried look on his face replaced with his smile. "Let's think on that." He stood and held out his hand.

My hand extended towards his and with ease, he pulled me to my feet. I said, "But the rest of it, the time off and vacation and stuff, that was all good." I reached down to pick up my notebook and pencil. "Let me write that down. Oh, and you said cash. Are we talking about going camping for a long weekend cash or tour Europe cash?"

Jeff walked up and put his arms around me. Simple vibrations of air went in my ear canal. "I love you more than you could ever comprehend, friend."

I reached my arms around him. "So, European?"

He placed his hands on my shoulders and pushed me back to arm's length. His eyes locked on mine. "Right now, I am anxious to meet your family. Can we get going?"

I nodded and he walked around the front of my car. I just watched him in wonder. Why was I with such an astounding being? He got to his door and looked over at me watching. He gave me a calm smile and answered the question I was asking myself. "The simplest way to describe it is, I talked to you from the fourth-dimension. From the human mind, it seems like it's from everywhere at once."

I nodded. "So, we're back to the book *Flatland*. You're the sphere talking to the square."

He opened his door and got in. I followed suit. Once the car was started he answered me. "It's all very complicated but the analogy from *Flatland* gets us pretty far. But the more important thing is what I said to you. Don't go home and start stressing about getting a job. We paid you way more than enough at HRI. Please just relax with the family. Just be Stanley."

I looked at him blankly. "Okay, I'll do that, and then what? At some point, I still have to get money coming in."

He looked at me hopefully. "Can you just trust me? Things will work out."

My blank look changed to a smile. "Yeah, I can trust you, Jeff. I'll take some time and be Stanley. But you have to explain that to Beth."

He held out his hand to shake. "It's a deal."

We shook hands and got back on the road.

Chapter 62

It wasn't but ten minutes later we pulled up to a red light on Route 58. I felt a coldness run through my veins as I stopped at the light. Jeff watched as I turned on my left blinker but didn't say anything. When the light turned green, I paused, looked both north and south for traffic. Nothing was coming, so I turned left and then a quick right into the gas station on the southwest corner.

I pulled into a parking spot near that corner and got out of the car, forgetting about my passenger. Instead, my mind was filled with visions of a motorcycle passing right in front of me at eighty miles-per-hour through a red light. The coldness continued to run through my veins as the image from our trip east play and replayed in my mind.

If Jeff hadn't told me to hit the brakes, my trip, and my life, would have ended at Kramer Junction that morning. I looked to my left at where my blue Jetta was sitting at the light that day. Then I looked north, up Route 395, where the bike came from. There was no way Jeff could have seen it. Yet he knew it was coming.

I felt his presence beside me. I softly said, "This was where you first showed me you were special. You saved my life."

I waited but he didn't respond.

I turned to him. "Messiah? Prophet? What?"

He shrugged. "Let's go with the 'what'. The other two titles are so loaded now. We could never get a useful meaning out of them."

"But you're Divine? I mean, sent by God."

Again, he shrugged. "Same problem. Like most people in America, you grew up in a Christian church with the Christian theology dominating your understanding of 'divine', your understanding of God, your understanding of the afterlife." He placed his hand on my shoulder. "We are the same, you and me. The only difference is, I've learned to see from a different place. I've learned this mind and body, which exists on this Earth, is not the sum of who I am. I've learned to connect to the me past this," he held up his hands and slowly turned, "existence." He paused and looked at me to see if I was understanding.

I returned the look and nodded. I felt like I should say something but nothing in my brain was triggering my mouth to move.

"Like others before me, once they learned to connect to their greater self, they tried to teach and guide others to a better way. What happened then, religions were formed around what they said and 'one-true-way' theologies were born. Christianity is stuck. It has lost its way. It is time to grow again. The waves have settled and new waves are being created."

I looked back to the intersection and then to the ground as I thought about what he said. "Lost its way. It has always felt like that to me." I looked back to him. "As much of pain as you are, you always make sense. I mean, the greater self part. Seems like that's what Harris was talking about with walls in his brain exploding or Deon saying parts of his brain started working."

Jeff grinned. "Even more than that. You're connected to a you much more powerful than your physical brain. But learning to blow up those walls in your physical brain is the first step to access that part of you."

"Vertical growth." I grinned back at my teacher. "There is a lot more vertical than I imagined."

Jeff put his arm around me. "We are gods, my friend. We only need to realize it and accept it." We both turned towards the Jetta. "So, Messiah or Prophet? Which do you pick?"

We separated and made our way to our respective doors. Over the car, I looked him in the eye. "I think 'friend' works best."

"Me too."

* * *

As the numbers on the signs giving the distance to Bakersfield grew smaller, I got more nervous and excited. The turns started becoming familiar, and the stores, parks, and restaurants started having a "not from some other place" feeling but instead, from my place feeling. Then, there it was. My home for the last eleven years came into view and my heart started racing. I pulled in the driveway and instantly the front door of my house flew open with a force I thought would take it off the hinges as Cooper cleared all three stairs on the porch with a mighty bound rushing to the car. Right behind him was the most beautiful six-year-old girl in the world, Alice. Then the beautiful woman who has put up with me for so long stepped out and smiled as she saw her kids, our kids, race with excitement towards me. Jeff was right, everything was going to be okay. I was home. I was where I needed to be. No matter what happened next, things were going to be okay.

I got out of the car, afraid I would take the door off the hinges, and raced with just as much speed to my kids and hugged them with as much love as I could fit into a hug. Beth stood there patiently waiting for her turn but wouldn't dare take the moment from the kids. When they showed signs of slowing down I stood and embraced Beth thinking of how wonderful it was to hold her.

She backed up and looked at me. "Stanley, how much weight have you lost? You look great."

"I don't know. I really haven't even thought about it." She pulled me in for another hug.

I glanced over at Jeff who was leaning on the open car door, watching with his never-ending smile. I led Beth and the kids over to him. "Jeff, this is my family, family, this is Jeff." It sounded like a simple statement but it carried a completeness I could never give words to. Two universes met and created one perfect one.

Beth walked up and hugged him. "Thank you for taking care of Stanley. He's told me so many wonderful things about you," were her first words to Jeff.

"I should be the one thanking you. He's a true blessing and I took him away from you guys for too long. We'll miss him at the Institute and I'll miss spending time with him but it's obvious this is where he needs to be," Jeff answered back.

Jeff got down on Alice's level and held out his hand. "Your dad can't stop talking about you. I think I already know everything there is to know about you."

Alice shook his hand. "Bet you didn't know I lost a tooth today."

My thought was, "I'll bet he did."

But Jeff just played it cool. "You got me there. I don't know everything about you." He turned to Cooper. "And I know a lot about you too. In fact, *The Change* sent me a couple of things to give you. They're packed away right now so I'll get them after we unload."

Cooper's eyes got wide. "*The Change* sent me something. That's so cool."

I interrupted. "So, let's grab an armload of stuff and go inside. Maybe Jeff can find it."

Once inside, the kids and I sat on the couch. Beth held out her hand offering Jeff a recliner to sit on and she took the other one.

It appeared there was going to be an uncomfortable silence but Beth didn't let that happen. "Glad you guys had a safe trip. No flat tires this time?"

Jeff shook his head. "No flat tires. The trip went about as I expected."

That made me smile inside. I'm sure the trip went exactly as he expected. That brought another thought. How much of the trip, there and back, was his doing? And HRI seemed tailored to suit me about perfect. How much of the trip was planned for me? From the time I checked the 'willing to relocate' button, Jeff's hand was manipulating my future. Most likely, even before. But why all the experience on the way?

Before I could explore the thought, Beth was talking. "How are you getting back? Do we need to get you to the airport?"

The question caught me by surprise. It had never occurred to me to ask him.

"Don't worry about me, I've made plans." He didn't answer the question and now that Beth had raised it, I was curious.

Beth nodded. "Well, I hope you didn't make those plans too soon. You're welcome to stick around as long as you want. I know it isn't the Ritz, but we have a hide-a-bed right here and we supply the entertainment with dinner."

There was something else I hadn't planned for. My plans stopped at getting home. How Jeff was getting home or how long he would stay never entered my mind.

Jeff gave an approving look. "I'll start my trip back tomorrow. The hide-a-bed would be great for tonight if you don't mind. And it's rare for me to not take an offer to share a meal with friends."

* * *

We made some more small talk. The kids seemed happy just to listen and sit next to me. My nervousness was gone. Everything was going to be okay no matter what. I would find a job doing something, anything, and come home to the greatest family a man could know. Thanks to the Institute's low-interest loan for the house and credit cards and all the overtime I got for the charity work, I was caught up on all of our bills and we had money saved up.

At a good break in the conversation, I told the kids to give me a hand unloading the car. Cooper was ready to go. He had been uncharacteristically patient about waiting for his gift.

I gave the kids their first load and they started toward the house. I asked Jeff the question that I should've asked a week ago, "So, how are you getting back?"

"I'll hitchhike," was his casual answer.

"I don't get that. You could fly, rent a car, teleport yourself, or whatever you call that. Why would you hitchhike?" I asked.

"You asked that when we first met. The answer hasn't changed. Where's the adventure in flying or teleporting? If I flew I'd sit by someone for a couple of hours and the trip would be over. If I teleport, it's even less interesting. I don't advise others to hitchhike or even pick up hitchhikers but it works great for me. The people I pick to ride with are people who need me."

"I almost feel sorry for the people who take you back," I said with a smile but thankful he got in the car at the start of my trip. At the same time, I felt a tinge of jealousy. Is this something he does all the time? Maybe my time with him was just another in a long line of people having an experience with him. Then I mentally kicked myself in the butt. So what if I was. If there was one thing I should have learned from this was, it isn't about me. "It'll take you about a week to get back. Doesn't your family need you?"

He replied, "I don't do this too often but it's good for them."

I was intrigued, "How so?"

"If you think about it, I'm an easy person to get dependent on. That's not good. Me being away helps reduce the dependency. My family's *need* is a place in our hearts and I'll always be in that place just as they will always be in that place in my heart. If I'm physically with them, they love having me around, but if I'm gone, they love having me in their heart. As far as the day-to-day activities, we have that covered. Jonathan's there, Grace is there, and all of the older kids help with the younger. We have the nurses and other caretakers who are just like any family member and they all help. Just like the Institute will function fine without me or any other single person, my family gets along fine. There's no single point of failure because in both the Institute and my family, whenever possible, everyone is involved in every aspect and will step up to make it happen. They also know when I'm gone, I'm gone for a good reason. I don't leave to get away from them."

"But they don't know who or what you are, so why would they think you're gone for a good reason?" I asked.

Jeff was loading some of my boxes in his arms. "They know I'm not a normal man and goodness follows in my path. They wouldn't be selfish enough to not want others to benefit as they have. So, it's true they don't know who I am by the definition of what humankind will say I am, but when that happens, they won't be surprised. Instead, the last puzzle pieces of their life with me will be in place and they'll be able to step back and see the magnificent, full picture. They'll never have witnessed any miracles, yet they'll still know I am what I am."

I was surprised by this. He must have performed miracles around them. "So, you don't do the teleporting thing and fourth-dimensional voice to others?"

He laughed at my question. "You're one of the very few who has knowingly witnessed anything like that and that's by plan. Jesus was plagued by people who wouldn't believe in him until they witnessed his miracles and many only came to see the miracles but still didn't believe. Witnessing miracles is no justification for belief, the message is the justification for belief. I don't walk around like a superhero ready to use my superpowers. I walk through life as a man, living as a man, to the greatest degree I can."

He lost me with that. As an avid fan of comic books, my train of thought was totally changed. "Superhero! That's a cool idea! You should do that. You could be 'The Messiah' or '5D man' and I'd be your sidekick 'Mr. Unemployed'. Well, we'll work on my name ..."

Jeff interrupted, "Stanley, come back. I should've known better than to say that. Drop the crime-fighting duo idea."

I saw the kids coming out for a second load and realized how much we had been talking. "Just have Beth tell you where to put that load and I'll load the kids up again."

In just a couple more trips we had the car unloaded. Cooper had another T-shirt signed by Marcus and a CD. He was already in the study listening to it. Jeff also had a couple of kids' books for Alice. I didn't even know he had brought anything for Alice but the books fit with his giving pattern and thrilled my daughter.

Beth had started dinner but wouldn't take any help, so Jeff and I went to the back patio by the pool.

Jeff looked around my backyard. "Nice place, friend." He pointed towards the back of the yard. "Looks like a good compost pile there."

I looked at it with an appreciation for my son. "Looks like Cooper's been keeping it going pretty good. Maybe we can grow a decent garden this time."

The conversation slowed down after that. I looked at him. "You know, tomorrow starts a different phase for us. You go back home to HRI and I'm here. I feel like I should be asking some questions while we're still in this phase. Would it be worth asking any direct questions? Would I get any answers?"

He looked at me and paused. "This is dangerous ground. What if I give you an unbelievable answer? Where does that leave you? Right now, you've seen some amazing things firsthand. You know they happened. You've seen a different way of life and a message to go along with it. You've become friends with this man named Jeff and you trust Jeff. Now, what if this Jeff gives you a direct answer and you can't accept it? And honestly, there's a very good chance you can't. What do you do with all you've seen and learned? You can attach it all to a benevolent mystery named Jeff but you can't attach it to an unbelievable fact much more magnificent and incomprehensible than Jeff."

I was trying to grasp what he was saying. "So, I've seen all these things and been told all these ideas which resonate with me, but you're saying, if you come straight out and tell me, I don't know ..." I tried to come up with an example of something unbelievable to me and it didn't take long. "Oh, I do know. If you come out and told me there actually is a man in the sky with a white beard looking down on us and judging us, then I would dismiss everything I've seen and everything you've said?"

He shook his head. "You went the wrong direction, friend. An anthropomorphic being is too simple of an explanation for you. That's the god you can't believe in. But go the other direction. There's a reason Jesus didn't talk about multidimensional beings. Cultures from the beginning of time have had anthropomorphic gods, so people could attach Jesus' message to that concept. His message would have been lost if people couldn't comprehend his true self, so he explained himself as honestly as he could in a way people could grasp. But now people are ready to understand a more complex reality."

This brought back the Kramer Junction conversation. "But not the whole reality. So, the waves from Jesus have calmed and you're creating the new waves of understanding."

He nodded. "And, when those waves settle, someone will come and move humanity to the next level of understanding."

I looked at the man named Jeff and wondered what I should ask him. Without a doubt, I trusted him and knew he was giving me a guideline. "But you're human, right?"

He moved his head affirming I was correct. "I told you earlier, you and I are the same. DNA from my mother and father. I was born just like everyone else."

"Why the adoption? Just to add to the mystery?"

He shook his head and stuck out his lower lip. "No, nothing like that. Just normal stuff. My biological parents couldn't raise a kid at the time. But I ended up in a pretty good place."

"You say that so matter-of-factly. Didn't it bother you, you didn't know your parents? I mean, you were a fairly normal person until you came back from your bike trip, right?"

He paused and thought. "I guess it bothered me some before I remembered who I was."

"Remembered who you are?"

Jeff nodded calmly. "I'm a god."

I gave him a questioning look. "You've said that twice today."

A gentle smile came to his face followed by a polite laugh. "You're a god, too. You don't remember who you are. I find it interesting Christianity doesn't teach that even with Jesus saying it."

"Jesus said that?"

"Sure. In John 10:34 Jesus says. 'Is it not written in your Law," I have said you are gods'"?"

I looked at him questioningly. "I've never heard that preached. Seems kind of major, doesn't it?"

He just nodded.

"How did you remember who you were? Did someone teach you?"

"It wasn't one thing or one person. I've always read a lot. That opens doors. My parents dying sent me in a tailspin which probably helped. After that, I talked to a lot of wise men and a lot of fools." He held up his finger toward me. "Don't discount fools. They have a lot to teach you. Learning to learn from fools is a powerful thing."

With a smile, I said, "I know. I've had a couple of months to practice."

He laughed out loud. "Yes, you have, friend. Yes, you have."

Beth walked out and somewhat sarcastically asked, "You weary travelers ready for dinner?"

"Yes, we are," I answered. Beth shut the door and I placed my hands on the arms of my chair and pushed up. "We're not weary travelers, we're gods."

He didn't smile. Instead, he looked me square in the eye and seriously said, "And tonight, we'll dine with the gods."

I wanted to laugh but Jeff was intentionally making the point he was serious.

Chapter 63

At my honorary place at the head of the table for my first meal back was my favorite meal sitting in front of me, Beth's awesome meatloaf. She puts bacon and salsa in it.

We all held hands and Alice led the prayer thanking God for me being home, Jeff being here, and a plethora of other things. It was such a joy to hear her again. I looked around thankful for my plethora of things. We were having a lively dinner with lots of laughing, talking, and Beth's wonderful food.

"This must be a calm dinner for you, Jeff," Beth said. "Stanley's told me about your dinners. They have to be an event in themselves."

"Oh, it's an event but it works out much better than you'd imagine when you hear about it without knowing my family. When you have that many people, everyone learns to step in where they're needed and it all gets done without any, or at least, without much complaining. But meals with the family are one of my favorite times of the day. It's where a lot of family bonding happens. I take any chance I have to sit with any family and eat a meal."

Beth then looked at me. "I was afraid you would come back with some extra weight from eating out or microwave meals, but you look great."

"I ate only the free breakfasts and lunches at the Institute. They were good but the nutritionist said they were also very good for you. For dinner, I did eat out or microwave dinners but also ate at Jeff's often. I think he has the same nutritionist because the meals seem a lot like the Institute's. I was also invited to almost every fitness group the Institute had. I've been playing racquetball, rock climbing, swimming, running, biking, and a bunch of other stuff. But I haven't thought much about my weight. Now that I'm thinking about it I just realized my pants are baggy."

Jeff added, "Think about all the people in the Institute, Stanley. Do you recall seeing any overweight people there?" Jeff made me think for a minute.

After thinking back, I realized he was right. "This doesn't make me feel very observant, Jeff. I hadn't noticed that at all, but there aren't any people who come to mind."

"That has saved us a fortune in health insurance. We can offer free food, free health insurance and still save money just due to the massive decrease in health care needs due to prevention."

Cooper spoke up. "In school, the teacher was talking about something like that. She said something about obesity and diabetes." I looked at him with pride. I was impressed he remembered the words and even more impressed he seemed to understand.

Jeff's smile showed he was impressed too. "He must take after his mom."

I smirked at him but didn't respond.

Jeff continued, "Ben Franklin said, 'An ounce of prevention is worth a pound of cure' and we're proof of that. Even with unlimited time off people are rarely out for illness. We've had to implement a minimum vacation policy."

Beth gave a short laugh. "You make employees take a vacation?"

"Yeah, normally three weeks but sometimes more. There's a strong connection between physical health and mental health. When you feel good physically, your mind works better and vice versa."

"I'm just thrilled to see a thin, sexy husband come home." Beth winked at me playfully as she said that.

Cooper made a gagging sound.

She's a beautiful woman. I missed her when I was gone but I was just starting to realize how much.

She continued. "And, it's nice to see the worry gone."

Before this line of conversation could go on, Cooper asked, "Can we play a game after dinner?"

"Sure, go pick one out after we get the table cleaned off," I answered.

The five of us sat at the table and played a couple of different board games with the kids until it was time for them to go to bed. They had school in the morning so, as much as I wanted to spend time with them tonight, they had to get to bed.

Beth, Jeff, and I stayed up and made small talk for a while. I was impressed with Beth's ability to be Beth. She also let the time with him be the time with him and didn't push questions on him or make a big fuss about him being here.

Now that I was home and the trip was over, I sat there on the couch fading fast. It had been a long two and a half months and I was ready to sleep in my bed. "Jeff, if you don't mind I'd like to reacquaint myself with my bed."

"I don't mind at all, friend. Don't worry about me, I'll be just fine." Jeff was a gracious guest.

Beth offered to make up the hide-a-bed. Jeff told her to just bring him the sheets and he would take care of it.

I came out when I was ready for bed just to make sure Jeff had what he needed. He had his back to me looking at books on the bookshelf. There was a mix of technical books, literature, novels, car repair manuals, reference books of all sorts. "Haven't you read all of those?"

Without turning to face me, "Not all of them, do you have any other books?" I lead him to the study which had even more.

"Help yourself, and if that doesn't keep you busy I can find more," I offered. "Anything else you need?"

With his infinite smile, he answered, "Nope. I'm set."

Once back in my bedroom, Beth was finishing up winding down and just getting in bed. I slipped in beside her and held her.

She talked quietly. "I wasn't sure what to expect with Jeff. I was nervous about him coming, but now it just seems right. I don't feel like I need to put on airs."

I smiled to myself and replied, "It would be pointless if you did."

"He has a power about him with his calmness. It's easy to sense greatness, but even more so, I can sense the love."

She was exactly right but I was fading and just wanted to be with her. "So, after two and a half months, your husband is in bed with you, and you want to talk about the guy on the hide-a-bed? If there's someone I want to sense right now, it isn't Jeff, it's you." As she drew in closer to me I smiled to myself as I held her tight but drifted off into a comfortable sleep.

Chapter 64

About four in the morning I woke up and was hungry. I laid there for a while trying to go back to sleep, hoping to forget about the hunger, but it was no use. Finally, I carefully got out of bed, so I wouldn't wake Beth up, went out of the room and down the hall with no lights on. There was a light coming from the living room so I stuck my head in there. Jeff was in the recliner with the lamp on next to him reading a book. I walked in and noticed the hide-a-bed wasn't pulled out and the sheets were still folded where Beth had set them. Jeff looked up from the book, a repair manual for an old Chevy truck I had sold years ago.

"That's one of the books you've never read?" I asked him.

"One of them. I've also never read the book on PHP and MySQL Web Development you have there. It was pretty interesting," he answered.

"You sit up and read repair manuals and programming books at four in the morning on things you'll most likely never do?

He was mockingly indignant at this point. "I may."

I looked back at the couch, "Have you even gone to sleep?"

"Well," he shrugged his shoulders and again with a mock look but this time of embarrassment, "I actually don't sleep. But it gives me a lot of time to read or do other stuff."

"What do you mean you don't sleep? You have to sleep. You would die without sleep."

"I meditate for about an hour or so but I don't actually sleep. I haven't needed to for a long time."

"All those nights in the hotels, you never slept?"

"Nope," was his simple reply.

"Why get a room?"

"Would you have understood when we're stopping for the nights? Would Beth understand if I told her I didn't need the sheets for the hide-a-bed? It comes across as weird."

I thought about that for a little bit and could understand where he was coming from. Especially on the trip to the Institute, when I first met him, he was already so bizarre. Him not sleeping would have been too much. "So, what do you do?"

"I read a lot. I have the shop at home, I can work out there. That's when I built the six-stroke engine for the Rolls. Since the internet, I've been able to find even more information easily. Could you imagine if Galileo or Copernicus or someone like that had the internet? What would they discover? There's so much information out there, just ready to be used."

I nodded in agreement. "It is hard for me to even remember how hard research for school papers use to be."

"When Ben Franklin was working on his theory on electricity, he communicated with other leaders in the field overseas by letters. Could you imagine what he would've done in modern times if he could have communicated with them instantaneously? And the open-source community, like your MySQL and PHP book there, or Linux, are great examples of the internet's potential. People who've never met face to face, working together to build software tools or software applications for the benefit of themselves and others. That's an amazing thing to see."

I had used a lot of that software in my career and agreed with Jeff, it was a pretty incredible thing. "Have you ever done any research on people who don't need sleep?" I said jokingly.

"There are documented cases ..." he started.

"I was just kidding. You hungry? I just got up to get something to eat." I invited him to my fridge.

"You bet."

We hit the fridge, pulled out stuff that looked like it shouldn't be eaten, and ate it.

We sat quietly eating for a little while as I wondered what I would do if I never slept. People complain that there aren't enough hours in the day but, if they had all twenty-four, what would they do? Bored people are a destructive force. I doubt many people would use the time to better themselves. Then I started wishing I had more faith in the human race.

"What kind of future does humanity have?"

"It has an outstanding future."

I shook my head. "I don't think so." I was about to start explaining why but then I stopped. Jeff knew all the problems of humanity. "I don't think so."

He folded his arms on the table and leaned in towards me. "Things are changing, friend. That never starts off well. But …"

I interrupted, "Starts off well? We've had wars from the beginning of recorded history. Does your 'starts off' start there?"

He gave a sincere nod. "Pretty much. Say five or ten thousand years, whatever age you want to give the age of civilization, is a blink of an eye. But we're at an important time of change and that will cause problems for a while. But you'll see people start to move to a new way of being. Different groups are talking about it in different ways but they're talking about the same change. Some talk about a change in vibrational levels. Some talk about an awakening. Some talk about the second coming. Whatever people want to call it; many people are moving towards the next stage of humanity. It is time."

His eyes were locking on mine and I couldn't help but be drawn into the magnificence they held and it made me feel so small.

I had to look away. "And the one bringing the change is sitting at my table. What sense does that make?"

He raised his hand as if to shoo away my words like they were a fly. "You've moved past being that Stanley. Stop using his language."

This caused me to look back at him and think about his statement. I thought about the days before the trip out there and how I was. Then I thought about my time at HRI, how exhilarating it was and how I know I contributed to its success. Then I thought about my open future. I wasn't scared, in fact, part of me was looking forward to Jeff going so I could start testing the new Stanley to see what he could do on his own.

My top teeth brought my lower lip into my mouth and I lowered my eyes as I thought about my next words. I knew what they were and I looked at Jeff with a knowing smile. "I'm ready for you to leave."

Jeff's face radiated with pride. "That's more like it, friend." He placed his hands on the table to stand and turned.

With a grin, I watched him walk to the kitchen doorway. "Not right now, bonehead. I'll kick you out tomorrow. You need to say goodbye to the family."

Without turning back, he said, "Good. I was just at the good part of the book. They're about to talk about rebuilding the automatic transmission. Talk to you in the morning."

With that, I headed back to bed to get a couple more hours of sleep.

* * *

I woke up to the smell of something cooking, looked over at Beth who was still in bed but starting to wake up. Her first words were, "That smells great."

I got some clothes on and headed down to find Jeff in the kitchen. He was doing some egg type of dish that looked and smelled great. He looked at me with his smile, "Hope you don't mind, I thought I'd make breakfast."

"I didn't see any eggs in the fridge last night."

"Yeah, I ran to the store while you guys were asleep," he replied.

"You found the extra keys okay?"

"No, I ran to the store."

With a confused look, I said, "The nearest store that would have been open is over five miles away."

"It was a good run, friend."

"You ran back with eggs?"

"Yeah, really makes you think about your stride."

I shook my head at him and didn't bother probing deeper into his choices in mobility. "What are you making?"

"It's a kind of soufflé," he answered. "I couldn't find soufflé bowls so it's in a baking dish. But it came out okay."

"Smells good."

Jeff was busy washing the dishes he used and looked over at me. "You guys were nice enough to have me as a guest so I thought I'd show some gratitude with a nice breakfast before the kids go to school."

Beth and the kids started showing up as we talked. Cooper went to the table and looked curiously at the strange breakfast. Cereal was the norm and on rare days, we had pancakes. "What's this?" he asked with a worried look on his face.

Jeff, with a French accent, said, "It is a sausage and egg soufflé, monsieur."

The accent didn't bolster any confidence with Cooper. "Is this some weird stuff? I don't like weird stuff."

Jeff looked at me with a smile and then back to my son. In a normal voice, "No Cooper, it isn't some weird stuff. I left out the ants and grasshoppers."

Cooper looked at it again. "Is it too late for the grasshoppers? I'd like to try those."

Alice was at the table ready to eat. She could care less what was in it. She would eat anything placed in front of her with no questions asked.

We all sat down and had an enjoyable breakfast talking about different insects and other strange things to make for our next meal.

Chapter 65

The meal couldn't last too long because school bells wait for no man. As we were loading our dishes in the dishwasher, Alice asked if I would take them to school. I started wondering about leaving Jeff and Beth. It seemed awkward but I didn't have time to think long on it.

Beth said, "I think that would be a good idea. You haven't had the chance in a couple of months."

This kind of surprised me and spoke to Beth's acceptance of Jeff. Leaving my wife with a man she had only known for a few hours seemed out of character for her.

I looked at her. "You sure? It ..." Then I tried to find a comfortable way to say what I was thinking.

Before I could figure out how to word the sentence Beth broke in and looked at Jeff. "I've known him for two and a half months. He's not a stranger."

Jeff pointed to the sink. "I still have some cleaning up from breakfast."

I shrugged. "Okay. Say goodbye to Mr. Havens, kids. He'll be gone before you get home."

Cooper extended his hand. "Bye, Mr. Havens, and thanks for playing some games and making the strange breakfast. Tell *The Change* thank you for the CDs."

Jeff lowered himself to Cooper's level. "I'll make sure to tell him, Cooper. It was a pleasure meeting you."

Alice went up to him while he was down on Cooper's level and hugged him. She said, "Thanks for helping my Daddy be happy. I like seeing him like this. Mommy said you're ..."

I stopped her. "That's enough, Alice." I didn't want to take the chance at what might come out.

Jeff returned her hug. "It's so good to meet you after all the nice things your dad told me about you."

Alice released him and went to the door. Cooper and I followed. We got in the car and started down the road.

"Daddy?" I looked in the rearview mirror at Alice. "I really like Mr. Havens."

Cooper's voice next to me moved my eyes from the mirror to him. "Yeah. He's different than other people."

This was a curious statement from an eight-year-old. "How so?"

He shrugged. "Don't know. Just seems like ... like ... he belongs."

"Hmmm." I thought about it for a few seconds. "That's as good of a way to describe it as I could come up with, Cooper."

We got to the school and I parked. I had only been to their school a handful of times. I had been to Rita's school in Bethlehem more times than I had to my own kids' school. Alice grabbed my hand and we walked to the front of the school. There were kids everywhere and adults trying to herd them to the designated areas.

"Good morning," a voice said as I walked with my kids.

I looked over. It was the principal I had met once or twice while I was here. I couldn't remember his name though. I took a few steps in his direction and extended my hand. "Good morning. I'm Stanley Whitmore." I looked down at my kids. "The father of these fine young people."

He reached out and took my hand with a firm grip and a friendly smile. "Phil Hampton. I'm the principal. Glad to see you here with them, Mr. Whitmore."

I echoed his name in my mind a few times to try to remember it. "Thanks, Mr. Hampton. I'd been out of town on business for a couple of months. Alice wanted me to bring them to school."

"Well, glad to see you here. If you want to stick around just check-in at the office. We like to have parents around."

He was a man you couldn't help but like. I remembered liking him the other time I saw him but now, I guess after spending time in Rita's school, I was looking at this school with new eyes. He struck me as a man who cared about the school and his invitation to stay was impressive. I'd always felt schools were unwelcoming places for me as a father but now I was coming to the conclusion it had more to do with my mindset than the school's policies.

I gave him a wistful look. "I can't today. I have to get back."

His look was polite. This was the response he was expecting. I'm sure it was what he was used to hearing.

I quickly added, "But I have some time off now. I'll come spend some time."

His face made it clear he had heard this before too. "Well, you're always welcome. Hope to see you soon."

We turned and walked to the doors. I stopped the kids and pointed up above the doors.

Cooper said, "Yeah, they put that up a little while ago. *The Change* sent the school the T-shirts and then *Invite The Change* stickers started being all over."

I turned back towards Mr. Hampton with growing respect. He didn't make the connection between me and the T-shirts. That was okay. I preferred it that way.

As I was thinking that, Mr. Hampton turned and smiled at me. Then he looked at the large sticker above the door and back to me. He snapped his fingers and I knew the connection was made.

He quickly walked over. "I knew I was forgetting something when we were talking. I apologize. My mind's all over the place every day and it's hard to keep everything in its proper place. Thanks for the T-shirts. They were a big hit. We're just starting to get going on the *Invite The Change* program. It's pretty exciting."

My shoulders rose a little. "That was Marcus' doing. But that's how he is. I just wanted a T-shirt for Cooper and the whole school gets some."

The bell rang and interrupted our conversation. He shooed me with his hands. "Get them to class. Hope we can talk later."

I got them both to class before the tardy bell and then walked in quietness to my car. From chaos to quiet in minutes just because a bell rang.

I headed home a little worried about leaving Jeff and Beth together. So far, she hadn't pushed him with questions and was just letting the time with him unfold as it may. In return, Jeff was a polite guest. It seems like it was just me he was out to torment in his loving way. Even Bear, Luke, and others were innocent bystanders in my torment.

When I got home Jeff and Beth were sitting in the living room talking. It didn't sound too involved. It sounded more like two old friends catching up on the past.

I sat on the couch next to Beth and the conversation was about to start again when Beth's phone beeped. She picked it up and looked at it with a bit of annoyance. "I forgot I had an aerobics class this morning. But I don't …"

Jeff interrupted. "I'm leaving pretty soon too. So, don't miss it on my account."

I smiled inside. Since we had a little money again, Beth had started up some of hers and the kids' activities. One of her favorites was an aerobics class. It was a good feeling to be able to provide for my family after months of cutting everything.

Beth gave Jeff a worried look. "Are you sure?" Before Jeff could speak she stood. "Actually, I'd be in the way. You two need that time without me. I just need to grab my stuff and I'll be gone."

Within minutes Beth had her gym bag and keys in her hand. As with the kids, I was surprised how quickly she'd taken to him. Her goodbye was like one given to a longtime family friend instead of a man she'd just met.

Beth was so very right about me needing this time alone with Jeff. I needed to say goodbye to the man who had given me gifts that turned my life upside down. Once he was gone I'd have to start my journey sorting everything out without him. This was a time I knew I needed and, strangely, found myself looking forward to.

I halfway jokingly asked him, "Where's my book?"

He looked over at me saying nothing.

I continued, "Seems like you've given everyone else you meet a book with a phone number to call you. I don't get one?"

He shrugged and then walked to a pile of his stuff. "It's not the same thing but I have the books I bought at George's I don't want to carry back. If it makes you feel better, I can write a number in them. But you're past me handing you a book and it transforming you. You know what to do and now is a time for Stanley to be Stanley. It's time for me to back off and let the waves settle." He watched my reaction which was surprisingly one of understanding. I knew it was time for me to reduce my dependency on him.

I moved on to the real thing bothering me. "You still aren't going to give me any clue as to what I'm supposed to do, are you?" I held up my hand. "And don't do that voice thing."

He grinned while he sat down and started putting a few things in his backpack. Then he handed me the suit he brought for the wedding. "This should fit you pretty well. I can't take it back with me."

He and I were close to the same size so I hoped it looked as good on me as it did him. Then he went back to answering my question. "What direction you thinking? Do you want me to help you come up with wording for your sign to start a street-corner evangelism campaign?"

I shook my head, "Nah, I have that figured out. I'll simply go with the old standby, 'The End is Near' and other stuff like that."

He grinned at my idea and zipped his backpack. "I can see that. It may work for you. Make sure to list some Bible verses too, like Ezekiel 23:20 and stuff like that."

"Thanks for the advice but I'm pretty sure street-corner evangelism isn't the direction I'm heading. I think we can safely count that one out along with becoming a minister. This leaves me with a short list of what I think I can do for you. The list now has zero items on it."

He was all packed with his backpack on the floor between his legs as he sat on the recliner looking at the floor thoughtfully. Then he looked up at me with a serious face. "I won't use the voice but I'll say the same thing I have been telling you for a long time. All you have to do is be Stanley. Take some time off before you start looking for a job. Take six or so months and just relax and enjoy time with your family."

I gave him a look of frustration. "That's no answer. That's no direction. You want something from me. What do you want?"

He held up his index finger and returned my look of frustration. "Number one thing I want from you, stop worrying about what I want from you. Yes, out of all the people in the world, I picked you to do something for me. If I told you what that was you'd try to do it like I wanted, wonder if it was good enough for me, and spend your time putting me into it instead of just being Stanley and doing what Stanley does." Very slowly and deliberately he said. "Just be Stanley. Period."

"But ..."

Loudly, "Just be Stanley!"

Defeatedly, I leaned back on the couch. "I have some money saved up now and I may be able to get it to last …"

Jeff interrupted, "I told Sam to hold off on the repayment of your loan for at least six months. Interest won't start until then."

I nodded approvingly. "Okay, that helps. But as long as it took me to get the last job I don't see how I can do that. I don't want to live like we were the months before the job at the Institute. I need to start getting money coming in."

"Money isn't the issue, friend. If you need money, I've got money. The issue is faith, Stanley, just have faith." He handed me an 8x11 manila envelope, smiling at me and look which could do nothing but give me faith.

I looked at him questioningly but he just smiled. My thoughts rushed back to the time of the lottery ticket and I did not want to relive that. I held the envelope for what seemed to be a long time and just looked at it, afraid to open it.

I started to break the seal, my heart started racing and I started sweating just like I did at the gas station when I was scratching off the gray boxes. I had the seal broken now and only had to work up the nerve to look inside. I took a deep breath, reached in, and pulled out the contents. Instead of searching the room for a trash can, I smiled. In my hand was the most incredible photograph which could possibly exist in the world. It was incredible because it couldn't possibly exist. When I had my emotional breakdown in my last days at HRI, Jeff transported me to the cliff at Zion National Park. The same cliff where we prevented Harris from jumping. It was a stunning sunset and I distinctly remember thinking about what a beautiful picture it would be. In my hands was that picture taken from behind us. Jeff had his hand over my shoulder while we looked at the majesty of the moment. That moment was alive in the impossible picture.

I had faith. There was only one requirement of me, be Stanley. I had time to just to be Stanley.

"Wow!" was all I could think to say so I said it again. "Wow!"

"My love for you is beyond comprehension, Stanley." Jeff walked up and gave me a long, warm embrace, picked his backpack off the couch, and turned to the door. I slowly followed him out and watched him walk down the sidewalk. As he turned to head down the street he turned back, smiled, and waved. I waved back and watched him walk away. I had no fear. I wasn't scared.

I knew things would be all right. I sat down on the porch and watched him until he was out of sight and then looked back at the photo for a long time. Then I sat there wondering, "How do I be Stanley? What does that mean?"

This story is concluded in Part 4, which will be available soon.

Book List

This is a list of books mentioned in part 3. Some of them are duplicates. Enjoy!

The Act of Will – Dr. Roberto Assagioli

Flatland: A Romance of Many Dimensions – Edwin Abbott Abbott

Siddartha – Hermann Hesse

Man's Search for Meaning – Viktor E. Frankl

A Tree Grows in Brooklyn – Betty Smith

Jubal Sackett – Louis L'Amour

Made in the USA
Monee, IL
17 January 2023

25456420R00095